FACTS OF LIFE

Also by **gary soto**

gary soto

FACTS OF LIFE

stories

Houghton Mifflin Harcourt

BOSTON   NEW YORK

www.hmhbooks.com

Text set in Minion Pro

The Library of Congress has cataloged the hardcover edition as follows:
Soto, Gary.
Facts of life: stories / Gary Soto
v. cm.
Summary: Children and teens from all walks of life deal with the dramas of growing up.
Contents: The babysitter—Capturing the moment—Citizen of the world—D in English—The
ideal city—Identity theft—Seeing the future—Where did I go wrong?—Wise Uncle Joe—You
decide.   1. Conduct of life—Juvenile fiction. 2. Mexican Americans—Juvenile fiction. 3.
Children's stories, American. [1. Conduct of life—Fiction. 2. Mexican Americans—Fiction.
3. Short stories.]
I. Title.
PZ7.S7242Fac   2008
[Fic]—dc22
2007035765

ISBN: 978-0-15-206181-4 hardcover
ISBN: 978-0-547-57734-0 paperback

Manufactured in the United States of America
DOC 10 9 8 7 6 5 4 3 2 1
4500334923

For Rita Rudolf
and Frank Valderrama,
teachers keeping pace with
the young people

CONTENTS

FACTS OF LIFE

Where Did I Go Wrong?

TO ERASE THE MEMORY of an embarrassing strike-out in a slow-pitch game, Mickey Cortez entered Lupe's Super, Super Mercado and splurged on a soda and a bag of chili-flavored CornNuts. His baseball cap, which he customarily wore with the bill turned back, faced forward. He needed all the disguise he could find. His spirits had fallen to the level of his dragging shoelaces.

His mind played back the pain of his failure. He grimaced as he recalled hurling down his bat. Then he had irrationally blamed the swirl of dust that kicked up just as he swung through the third pitch and ended the game, 5–4.

"Stupid dust!" he had yelled. He scrubbed his eyes to make his point. But his teammates, who had been clinging hopefully to the chain-link fence, just groaned and began to gather their equipment.

Now, to make himself feel better, Mickey bought food and drink. The owner of the store was a friend of his father's, so the boy was allowed to ignore the scrawled sign above the magazine rack that read: BUY THE MAGAZINE—DON'T JUST READ IT.

He was eyeballing the latest issue of *Lowrider* magazine when a man whispered, "*Oye,* kid, you need work?" Mickey jumped, startled not by the man breathing down on him—and the fact that he was tattooed to his throat—but by the word he despised most of all. *Work. As in pick up a shovel?* he thought. *As in weed the flower bed? As in get an old towel from the garage and wash the car?*

"What?" Mickey asked weakly. "Did you say . . . work?"

The man's eyes were small in his large face, but that was the only thing small about him: He was barrel-chested, with muscle-packed shoulders and huge arms and legs. He stood just a few inches taller than Mickey, but much mightier.

"Yeah, kid, I'm looking for someone to help me move things. I'm paying good—thirty dollars—if you can spare a couple hours."

The man had to retrieve items from his grandfather's house. Old Gramps, the man quipped, had eaten too much *menudo* in his time and had suffered a heart attack. He touched his heart, and then the gold dollar sign that dangled from a large gold chain around his neck.

Mickey, seeing that this *hombre* was connected to a larger economy than the two quarters in his own pocket, became interested. At home he slaved for nothing—or next to nothing, just a dollar or two. Now this man was offering Mickey thirty bucks.

"How long will it take?"

"Not long," the man answered. "You're a strong-looking dude."

Mickey inflated his chest and held the air as long as he could before slowly releasing it. "Okay," he agreed.

He finished his soda and crushed the can in his fist, which made the man whistle and say, "You're strong, I'm telling you." Mickey smiled proudly and again inflated his chest.

Soon Mickey was in an old squeaky truck moving down Fruit Street. He noticed the radio was gone. "Your truck get jacked?"

"What?"

Mickey pointed at the cavern full of loose wires.

"Yeah," the man muttered, head shaking in disgust. "These be bad times. People just taking what they want." He scratched a tattoo that read BORN TO LOSE on his bicep. "But you know what the worst theft is?"

Mickey shook his head.

"It's when someone steals your soul."

Profound, Mickey thought. *The dude sounds like my dad when he's kicking it in his recliner and complaining about the government.*

The man introduced himself as Raul.

"I got a friend at school named Raul," Mickey said. "Him and me want to start a rock group."

"Is that right?" Raul asked. "What instrument you play?"

"Nothing right now, but we're going to learn."

"I'm sure you're gonna make it. And if not in music, then in sports. Bet you play ball, huh?"

Mickey beamed. "Yeah, actually, I play slow-pitch." His recent outing, he figured, had been a fluke. The stupid dust messed him up—dust and everyone looking at him from the dugout.

Mickey spied a car approaching from the opposite direction. It was his father's car. A zipper of fear ran up his back. What would his father think of his son in a truck driven by a total stranger? He was only thirteen. Or would his father be proud that he had found work?

"Is this place far?" Mickey felt nervous. "My mom likes me to be home by five." He caught sight of a tattoo in Lowrider script, carlos, on the guy's wrist. *Which is it?* Mickey wondered. *Raul or Carlos?*

"Nah, it's just right around here," Raul answered.

The truck turned a corner. They were in a nice part of their small city, with flowers standing up in well-fertilized soil and sharing their pretty faces with passersby. Automatic sprinklers were spinning out water on supergreen lawns.

"It's one of these," Raul said. He peered out the windshield splotched with the horrible deaths of insects.

Mickey was certain his widowed aunt lived on this street. Her husband had died while ordering a hamburger. This was just about all he remembered about his uncle, a baker who went to bed before the good television programs started and got up while it was still night.

Raul searched for a house, braked, backed the truck up a few feet, and crept into the driveway, cutting the engine and letting the truck roll until it stopped. The house was near the corner, and its lawn sparkled from a recent soaking. A flag with smiling bunnies and turtles on it hung by the door.

"Your grandfather lives here?" To Mickey, the house didn't seem very Mexican, and Raul, dark as a penny, was *puro* homie.

"That's right. You wait here 'cause I got to go around the back and get the key." Raul jumped out of the truck and disappeared through a gate at the side of the house.

Mickey wrote his name on the dusty dashboard, then leaped from the truck. Before he slammed the door, he noticed six or seven cell phones under the passenger's seat, maybe more. Was Raul a thief?

"Dang," he whispered. Was he, a tender seventh grader, being pulled into a crime that would send him to juvie until he was seventeen? By then, his voice would have deepened like a frog's.

Mickey didn't dwell on this question because Raul had appeared on the porch. "Come on, champ," he called with a wave. Somehow, Mickey couldn't disappoint this guy—he was sort of cool with all his tattoos.

Once inside the house, he was greeted by cool air, a tidy living room, and bright artificial flowers in a vase. Raul closed the door behind them and pointed to a huge television. Mickey whistled. It could have been an altar in a church because a cross and a picture of Jesus sat on top.

"We're going to move this?" Mickey sidled up to the television and perceived that it was taller than he.

"Yeah, that's why I need you, champ." Mickey sensed Raul was trying to stroke him with a compliment. Still, he wasn't about to confront him and ask, "Hey, dude, you a thief? How come you got a tattoo that says Carlos?"

It was just too late.

Raul unplugged the television, tossed the cross and picture of Jesus onto the couch, and started to wrestle the TV from the wall. Together they moved one end, then the other, and walked the monstrous television across the living room to the front door. During this straining effort Mickey laid his eyes on framed photographs on the wall. One was of an elderly white couple, and below them were photographs of pinkish children. A flood of sweat sprang to his face. The zippers of fear went crazy on his back.

Face moist with sweat, Raul pulled at the front of his tank top and fanned himself. "Go get me a soda."

"What?"

"In the kitchen. Grab me and you a cold one." Raul

pulled out a white handkerchief and ran it across his face and neck.

It's stolen, Mickey reckoned. *The handkerchief belongs to the old man in the picture.* Raul was not the kind of guy who carried an ironed handkerchief white as snow. He must have cased the place—were the old folks on vacation?—and broken in, discovered a huge television on which to watch the Raiders in the fall, and recruited a naive soul in the shape of a thirteen-year-old strikeout king.

Be cool, Mickey reminded himself. He did what Raul asked and fetched two sodas. "Your grandfather is he, like, going to get better?" A split second later, he wished he could pull in that sentence like a fishing line. Why did he ask it?

Raul leveled a mean, snakelike stare at Mickey. The moment was so quiet that he could hear a leaky faucet drip in the kitchen.

Raul softened and answered, "Yeah, *mi abuelito* is gonna get better. The guy is strong, you know. He served in Nam and came back to pick grapes for fifteen years. Can you believe that?" He burped and added that his grandfather was a swell fellow who would give the shirt off his back.

"Times was hard then, huh?" Mickey thought of his own Mexican-born grandfather, who, according to family lore, walked five miles through a sandy desert to get to school. His grandfather, often lit with drink, reminded them every Christmas that he'd only gone up to eighth grade. He wanted his grandchildren to study hard and get jobs in office buildings where the air conditioning was free.

"You got that right, homie." Raul downed his soda, tossed the empty can on the couch, and ordered, "Back to work. Got that twenty dollars waiting for you."

Miffed that Raul had lowered his pay, Mickey nearly braved correcting him. He would need the full thirty dollars to buy the aluminum bat he had eyed at Big 5.

But even more, he wanted out! He debated whether to sprint out the front door, screaming his fool head off, "Thief! Thief! Help me! Somebody help me!" He pictured himself running in slow motion, the way he did in dreams in which he was hauling as fast as he could to first base. He feared that Raul would chase him down. What would his headstone read? thirteen-year-old struck out in the first inning of life!

By the time they got the television down the steps and into the back of the truck, both were sweating. "Is that all?" Mickey asked. "You know, I could walk home from here." He pasted a smile on his mug. He spanked his palms together to portray a kid done with work.

"No, I need you to come and unload it. Wait here." From the porch Raul turned and pointed a warning finger. "Don't go anywhere! That ten dollars is going to be yours."

He's lowering my pay again! Mickey's jaw dropped in disbelief. Raul *was* a cheap thief.

The smart part of Mickey's brain advised, *Run, sucka! Get your* nalgas *outta there!* He took off, his arms chugging away, but he could swear he was running in slow motion. He looked back: Raul was nowhere in sight.

I'll be good, he promised himself. *I will, really!* He swore he would cut the lawn when his dad asked and take out the garbage without making a face. He would wash the car properly, not just run a hose over the windshield. He'd even go to church. Yes, church! He would go with his mother and grandmother and not complain when they stayed for coffee hour.

Mickey was cutting across the street when he heard his name. "Mickey! *Mi'jo!*" Confused, he slowed to a stop, sweat filling the folds in his neck. Who was calling him?

It was Aunt Ester. She was in her side yard holding a pair of hedge clippers. He scampered to her, grateful for his good luck. He leaned over, hands on his knees, and tried to catch his breath. He had always considered his sprinter friend, Miguel Sanchez, an overrated athlete since he only ran a hundred meters. But he could see now that he was wrong. He had dashed no more than fifty yards and he was exhausted.

"Are you okay?" his aunt asked. "What are you doing around here?"

"I was . . ." Mickey stalled for a second, but then told his aunt that he'd been playing baseball with a friend.

"You look so red. You want something to drink?"

"Yeah," he answered.

His aunt waved to the backyard, where the hose was coiled. He would have groaned about her stinginess, but he was grateful for the safety of her yard.

Who cares? Mickey reflected. At this point he would drink mud! He was safe; he was alive! He drank from an old hose wrapped in places with cloth, then washed his face and neck.

"Would you like some lunch?" His aunt sidled up to him.

"Nah, I'm okay," he answered. "I really got to go, Auntie."

She pouted. "Oh, shoot. I thought maybe you could help me do something." She shaded her eyes and looked at the roof. "I was cleaning the yard, but I can't get up there. Can you sweep up there? The roof?"

"Sweep the roof?" Mickey questioned. His aunt was a certified clean freak and was known to skate around her polished floors on towels to protect the shine. Now was she taking her craziness outside and to a new level?

"Really, Auntie, I got to go." He took a step backward, the water in his stomach sloshing.

"*Mi'jo,*" she sang. "I'm fifty-four. I'm old. I have nobody."

Mickey found himself leaning a ladder against the side of the house, troubled because the day was not going as planned. All he'd wanted was a good day of slow-pitch, a quick dunk at his friend's house, and an hour or two of Game Boy before dinner. But the day had its own bag of tricks.

"My mom's going to kill me if I fall off the roof and die," he muttered.

At first he walked ducklike, but finally wobbled to his feet. He breathed in the air, and let the summer breeze play with his tangled hair. The world seemed so different at that height. He took a few cautious steps, then nearly fell off the roof when he spotted Raul walking up the street.

"He's gonna get me," Mickey whispered as once again he assumed a ducklike stance. His heart beat as fast as a rabbit's. He was glad that he had drunk like a camel because there was no telling how long he would have to remain on the roof.

"Don't forget to get around the chimney, *mi'jo*," his aunt instructed from below.

"I won't," he retorted in falsetto. He was glad his aunt hadn't called him by name. Raul might have heard it and, a gangster with time on his hands, would have waited for Aunt Ester to disappear into the house before he climbed the roof and got him.

Mickey moved to the other side of the roof, away from the street, and began to sweep, counting the strokes: twelve, thirteen, fourteen. He counted to fifty and then peeked over to the front part of the house. Raul was nowhere to be seen.

He finished sweeping the roof, descended the ladder, and herded the leaves, sticks, and pinecones into a trash can. He lugged the can to the alley, carefully unlatching the gate and peering out for fear that Raul was lurking there.

Mickey returned to the back porch and peered through the screen door into the kitchen.

"Auntie, I'm finished," he called, but not too loudly.

His aunt rewarded his labor by presenting him with a sandwich in a paper towel. He was glad for a meal, as the chili-flavored CornNuts had long ago been destroyed by his digestive juices. His stomach growled.

But when he peeled back the bread, Mickey saw only tomato—no meat, turkey or baloney, no cheese, no swipe of mayonnaise or mustard, or even a single leaf of lettuce. However, he assessed a sprinkling of salt and pepper the color of his father's five o'clock shadow.

"You're a growing boy," his aunt remarked.

"Looks tasty," he chimed. *Dang, she's cheap,* he brooded as he bit into the sandwich. Still, it was better than nothing. He devoured the sandwich in three bites, wiped his face with the napkin, and said, "That was good, Auntie. Gotta go."

Mickey left by way of the alley. The first thing he did was saucer his Dodgers cap into a trash can, disturbing the flies bulking up on nasty garbage.

"Good-bye, cap," he sang remorsefully. He had fond memories of it, but was savvy enough to realize it was a dead giveaway: Raul would be driving around in search of a boy in such a cap. He peeled off his Bart Simpson T-shirt, as this, too, was a giveaway.

"Dang," Mickey whispered. He imagined himself stripping off all his clothes and arriving home naked; his laugh came out like a snort. But his mirth fled when he came upon a cop's cruiser idling at the corner.

"Aw, man, I'm busted," he muttered. He stopped in his tracks, wondering how to escape. The rabbit inside his heart began to run. When he was eight years old he'd been nabbed by a cop who'd caught him scratching his name in wet cement. Was a boy ever so dumb?

He crept back into the alley, glancing now and then over his shoulder. Ratlike, he scurried down the alley and saw, not a light at the end of the tunnel, but another idling cop car.

"It's messed up," Mickey told himself. "But just be cool." He sauntered into view, seemingly relaxed as he whistled *"Cielito Lindo."* He picked up a stick and demonstrated, in a corny manner, his swashbuckling skills as a buccaneer: jab, jab, parry. Dramatically, he wiped his brow, as if to indicate the heat of the day. He had to convince the cop that he was only a sunstruck youth, and harmless.

Out of the corner of his eye, Mickey eyed the cop.

The cop's sunglasses turned in his direction, a glare sparkling. But he didn't roll down the window to ask, "Kid, you know anything about a break-in?" He remained in his air-conditioned cruiser.

He's probably just doing paperwork, Mickey figured. *Cops are always parked with their engines running and using good gas just to kill time.*

Mickey made his way down the street, tempted to turn and see if the cop was eyeing him with suspicion. But he kept himself looking straight ahead, not backward at that narrow escape, which he hoped would be a lesson in life—if he really *did* escape. He felt sorry for the old couple whose house he had helped rob. *If only I could do something for them,* he cried in his heart. But what? Arrive with a mower and cut their lawn?

Mickey walked, shoulders hunched. His favorite baseball cap was gone and so was his Bart Simpson T-shirt. *Dang, I'm almost naked,* he realized.

The day had started off so nicely with three bowls of Coco Puffs and continued with a bag of pork rinds as he walked to the baseball field. Yes, that's where it had all started, when he struck out and his teammates' angry stares became death rays.

"That stupid dust," Mickey snarled. But at least that was in the past, he figured.

But he was wrong there, too. The past came upon him when he spotted a member of his team bicycling toward him. It was Jesus Lopez, the guy he left stranded on second, and Jesus got bigger and bigger as he approached. He skidded to a halt, tossed a handful of sunflower seeds into his mouth, and asked, "Dude, how come you struck out?" He spit out the shells at Mickey's feet.

"You saw what happened!" Mickey's arms flapped like wings. "It was the dust. And quit spitting sunflower seeds at me."

"You messed up," Jesus sneered. "Get on."

Mickey was glad for the magical appearance of Jesus. On the handlebars of the bike, he could increase the distance between himself and the scene of the crime, plus the police.

At Jesus's house, Mickey helped pump up an inflatable pool and fill it with water from two garden hoses. "This is great!" He happily ripped off his shoes and socks, but kept his pants on as he stepped into the pool and sat down. A few bubbles rose around him like suds.

"Man, you were supposed to hose off first," Jesus complained as he stepped into the pool. "You're going to get the water all dirty."

"My germs are healthy." Mickey sighed, and splashed like a baby.

Jesus's younger brother and a friend appeared. Their necks were ringed with dirt from hard play.

"Let us in," Jesus's brother demanded. The corners of his mouth were blue from eating a Popsicle.

"Get outta here!" Jesus shouted. "And take your friend with you."

"Yeah, go play in the street," Mickey joined in as the two younger boys left.

The boys were having fun listing all the food they would never eat, even if they were starving on a deserted island, when a bubble rose and popped in front of Mickey.

"Did you fart in the water?" Jesus asked. He stood up, a sheet of water spilling off his brown body.

"Nah, man, I didn't! I swear." Mickey laughed. "But I did pee!"

Jesus was out of the water, and then Mickey was up and out, his belly rolling with laughter. "It was just an air pocket from my pants. I swear. And I didn't stream in your pool. It was just a joke."

"You farted! You disgust me! Now I gotta change the water."

Refreshed, Mickey dripped and savored the chills running across his body. His jeans clung to his thighs. He was still chuckling as he searched for his shoes.

"Where are they?" He found his socks, so dirty they were black as night.

Jesus turned in a circle, also puzzled. "I don't know, dude." Then he raised his face. "My little brother. I'm gonna kick his butt."

They went to the front yard and found the shoes, laces knotted together, dangling from a telephone wire.

"Your stupid brother!" Mickey scowled.

"Don't worry, I'll get him for you. And his big-nose friend."

They stood in silence as they gazed up at the shoes. But there was no way to get them down, and Mickey knew he had to go home.

He arrived home nearly naked and with a blister on each foot as proof he'd traveled far beyond the confines of his own block. He felt much richer in life, and wiser. His father greeted him.

"Heard you were over at your aunt Ester's," he reported from a chair on the porch. "Heard you helped her do something on the roof." He rubbed his stubbly chin and inquired about his son's clothes.

"Yeah, Dad." Mickey gazed down at his absence of apparel and offered, "It's a long story."

"I got no time for a long story." His father blasted his prodigal son, asking how he could walk five miles to help his aunt but not pick up the dirty clothes in his bedroom. "In fact, go get some clothes on, and come outside."

Mickey snuck inside to avoid his mother in the kitchen. When he opened his bedroom door, he discovered his father was partially right. There were clothes on the floor, and a sock—how did it get there?—hanging from the overhead light. He snatched the sock, found its mate under the bed, put on an ice-cream splattered T-shirt, and pushed his feet into tennis shoes. He went outside.

"What do you want me to do?" Mickey asked.

"You were monkeying around on your aunt's roof, and now you're going to do the same here." His dad handed him what, at first, Mickey thought were seat cushions. They were cooler pads.

For the second time in a day he was up on a roof, this time with a screwdriver in his back pocket. He opened the side of the cooler and detached the old pads, black as a smoker's lungs, and fit the new ones in. He stepped to the edge of the roof and dropped the old pads to the ground.

"That's all done," Mickey said proudly, a mustache of sweat on his upper lip. He moved toward the ladder, flipping the screwdriver into the air. "I'm pretty good at this," he claimed, seeing himself as a sort of circus act. He tossed the screwdriver higher and higher—and then, out of the corner of his eye, he made out Raul's truck on the street, tailpipe popping.

"Aw, man," Mickey sputtered.

The screwdriver flew out of his hand, and stuck in the ground within inches of his father, who was gathering mint from around the faucet in the flower bed.

"What the heck!" his father scolded. He hitched up his pants with both hands as he stepped back to locate his son on the roof. "Tryin' to kill your *papi*?" His father bawled him out in Spanish, but Mickey was deaf to his father's wrath. He stepped farther back on the roof, his heart racing, and squatted into the familiar ducklike stance. The back of Raul's truck was empty. He must have unloaded it and was making his rounds in a new neighborhood.

Earlier in the summer Mickey had begged his father to get a plasma television, but his father, a penny-pincher, had waved him off. Now Mickey was glad. Raul, a clever thief, would have sniffed out the television and made an unannounced visit. There Mickey would be, kicking back on the couch, three empty cereal bowls on the coffee table, his parents gone. Raul would push himself into the house, singing, "Hey, champ, long time no see. So this is your crib." He pictured Raul swiveling around and pointing, "Hey, nice TV, the latest in technology. Come on, help me carry it out."

Perish the thought that he, the prodigal son with blisters on his soles, would help rob his own house. Mickey remained on the roof until the truck disappeared and his father slapped open the front screen door, shouting, "Come on down, *mi'jo*. You've done enough for today."

Capturing the Moment

AS THE SCHOOL BUS bumped over the road, Lisa
Torres did a quick sketch of her classmate, Gaby Lopez.
Lisa, holder of two blue ribbons from the art contest at
the county fair, was inspired by the moment: a classmate studying the rain-wet fields of February. Lisa felt
that she had caught Gaby's pensive mood as she gazed
out the bus window. The high clouds had darkened the
landscape, the shadows racing east toward the Sierras,
the jagged range of mountains tipped with snow. Any
other day the valley's smog would have obscured their
view.

Lisa got up and moved unsteadily down the aisle.
The next stop was hers. "Here," she said to Gaby.

Surprised, Gaby accepted the portrait, and offered a smile. Her friends huddled around to look at the drawing and made Lisa think of ponies peering through a stall—would that be another sketch at another time?

The bus groaned to a stop in the middle of the road. Lisa lived out in the country where few cars passed. When they did, they sped by, far faster than the posted fifty-mile-an-hour sign, as if hurrying to get away. Lisa had spent many summers sitting in a chair counting the cars: one car every hour, sometimes stopping to ask for directions. City people, Lisa learned, didn't know east from west, and couldn't name the crops growing in the nearby fields.

Lisa shrugged her backpack onto her shoulder, descended from the bus, turned to wave at Gaby, and slowly walked up the muddy drive toward her trailer house set fifty feet back but visible to everyone. To Lisa, the trailer said "Poverty." The trailer said "Isolation." The trailer said "People live there, but why?" Lisa and her parents had called it home since crossing from Mexico six years earlier, leaving behind her two older brothers, a sister Lisa hardly knew, uncles and aunts, grandmothers, and a pony. Before they arrived in California, an excited Lisa had imagined places like Disneyland and movie theaters large as churches. She imagined herself eating at McDonald's every day. Her parents would drive something fancy, like a Lexus or a Mercedes.

She soon learned the truth: Some people have to live in the middle of nowhere. They eat dust, they scorch under the sun, they whittle away the hours in boredom. They drive an '83 Ford Ranger with mismatched front fenders. But most of the time Lisa didn't mind.

She leaped over a puddle, then another. She stooped to look at her reflection. She considered nature a better portraitist than her favorite artist, John Audubon, the genius who had drawn hundreds of birds. She had become familiar with this naturalist—a new word for her, a word she loved—when her dad found a book abandoned at a Laundromat. Audubon was a master artist, and his subjects were birds surrounded by sprigs of foliage, a leathery branch, or a small flower.

Lisa could see that her reflection, even in a puddle in her rural yard, had captured the moment. Even on this ugly plot of land, nature was a better artist than Audubon.

I want to go far away, Lisa thought, *and draw and draw. That's going to be my life.* She had heard about New York City—the Big Apple. That was where artists went to suffer for their art. If she had to suffer as well, she figured that she would do it in a large city—provided the suffering didn't involve scars and bruises.

Lisa smiled at her reflection, then made a funny face. She wore a cap, and her long hair blew in the wind. Her cheeks were pinkish from the cold and the wind, and her nose was moist. Lisa stepped away from nature's mirror and was debating what after-school snack she would fix when she spied a lake of rainwater that extended from their squat trailer to the rusting tractors parked in the back.

"Oh, wow," she remarked. The afternoon glare off the lake made her squint. *How strange,* she mused. It had rained just after lunch at school, but the downpour hadn't seemed that heavy. Had a cloud stalled above their trailer and poured out its little heart?

She strolled around the new lake, occasionally gazing back at her footprints in the soggy earth. The chickens in the yard were soggy, too, their feathers parted and showing the yellow skin underneath. Still, they scratched and pecked at the ground and left their own shallow prints in the wet earth.

I'll draw the lake, Lisa decided. She liked drawing birds, but had grown tired of sparrows, blue jays, and blackbirds wrapped in glossiness. These days she liked doing portraits, though she could draw objects, too.

The previous week she had drawn the pile of tires behind the tractors; the drawing now adorned the front of the refrigerator.

Lisa produced a pencil and her sketch pad from her backpack. She had to capture this lake before it disappeared into the earth, taking with it the fluffy clouds mirrored on its surface. Birds the color of asphalt flittered about the edges of the puddle, and she recognized them as common finches. She knelt on the wet ground, putting down on paper what her eye beheld, what her fingers were able to portray.

Her gift was a mystery, as neither of her parents could draw. Their talent was to bring their faces together, like lovebirds, and warble Mexican songs, although most of the time they were working. Her father was employed by a dairy and her mother, from windy March to scorching July, worked in the fields—she thinned beets and cotton and was sometimes on a women's crew that harvested cantaloupes. There were also two seasons when she packed peaches.

Lisa's dog, Pecas, roamed in the background. He paused, head raised and fur parting from the wind. Lisa had to smile. He seemed to be posing as the subject of her artwork. His breath hung in the air when he barked at movement in the grass—a rabbit, she wondered, or a quail in search of a mate? The gopher that had tunneled under their garden patch last summer and nibbled at everything her father had planted: cucumbers, tomatoes, chilies, and eggplant?

I'll surprise my parents with this new drawing, Lisa thought. *"Cállate!"* she ordered Pecas, who turned, head lifted and tail wagging, and happily trotted toward her. But when two large white birds dropped from the sky, Pecas lurched in fear, kicking up water. "Oh my gosh," Lisa uttered, dropping her pencil. She searched the sky for other birds. But the sky was vacant, except for blackbirds wheeling over the fields across the street.

As she took a cautious step toward the birds, she remembered that the night before she had been looking in her Audubon book at a picture of a bird that she would like to draw: the egret. Now before her stood a pair of egrets, which, against the backdrop of the grayish lake, were white as snow.

Lisa's heart thumped with excitement and Pecas's tail wagged briskly. Lisa again turned her attention skyward: Where had they come from? What wind had brought them *here* at this moment? She reached for the pencil on the ground and rolled it between her palms to spark the fires of creation. She had to draw these rare and silent birds, who, if she remembered right, seldom whistled or twittered with song.

Lisa turned and gasped. Over the lake arched a rainbow that began somewhere behind the tractors. The centerpiece was the pair of egrets, still as statues. Even Pecas stopped his whining. Lisa wondered, *Can he really see the rainbow?* She had read that dogs were mostly color-blind, but that birds, even common ones like the sparrow and finch, could slice the color red into a dozen shades. Their world was richer in color than some of the greatest paintings.

Lisa tried to sketch the scene quickly before it disappeared: First the egrets would fly away, then the rainbow fade, and finally the deposit of rain sink into the earth.

"It's so beautiful," she remarked.

A black-and-white calf ambled out from between the rusty tractors. Splattered with mud, it moved with a heavy sway toward the water. The calf stopped, then raised its heavy head to Lisa, as if saying, "Go ahead— draw me." It lowered its gaze to turn and present a mournful profile, spittle hanging from its mouth.

"Oh," Lisa let out, and added the cow to the scene. She made a face when she heard the telephone ring.

"Como lata!" Lisa muttered. She got to her feet, knees dimpled with mud, and hurried to the trailer with her sketchbook pressed to her chest. She petted Pecas's head as she bounced up the steps, slipped off her muddy shoes, then got the telephone on the fifth ring.

"Bueno," she greeted the caller. "Hello." It was her mom calling from the Laundromat—Lisa could hear the sound of tumbling dryers and washers shifting into rinse and spin cycles. She could make out the wailing of babies and Mexican music echoing off the walls. Her mother asked Lisa to take some frozen meat out to thaw, then to vacuum and clean up around the trailer.

Lisa hung up and looked around their small living room. In the corner stood her father's metal cabinet of Craftsman tools, which gave the air the faint scent of motor oil. Lisa's father, who'd been a truck driver in Mexico, had an ambition that would take them away from this trailer life. He wanted to become a mechanic. Mechanics earned good money, he argued, and they got to live in cities, not on *ranchos.* They got to drive clean cars, not ones flecked with mud or splattered insects on windshields. They owned tools, droplights, extension cords, and books with oil-thumbed pages.

My papi *is trying,* Lisa told herself. Still, she frowned at this tool cabinet that took up so much room; her frown deepened at her mother's knitting piled on the coffee table. Lisa hated herself for this judgment, but the house was messy, and no matter what she might do, it would always be messy.

Lisa released a sigh, and muttered, "I'll clean it later." She was determined to complete her drawing. She slipped into her shoes on the porch and clopped down the steps, then halted. Would surprises never end! Near the egrets under the rainbow's arch floated two fat geese.

Kneeling at the edge of the lake, Lisa quickly added to her penciled scene and noted the colors that she would employ later. As the light faded, the rainbow began to die. The calf turned and moved away in slow, plodding steps. The egrets unfolded their wings and spread them like accordions; they leaped into the air, their departure rippling the surface of the lake. The geese treaded out of the water, throwing hateful looks at the chickens in the yard. The chickens pecked the ground.

The moment, Lisa knew, was over. "Don't go!" she screamed to the egrets. She rose to her feet. "Don't go! Stay!"

But the egrets were soon dark commas on the western sky. Lisa watched until they were no longer visible. She shivered, and when she turned back to the lake of rainwater, the rainbow had vanished. The calf had ambled off to the pasture across the country road, where it nibbled on grass. In a few minutes it would blend into the dusk.

Lisa stood for a moment in the gathering dark. Daylight began to pull west, and the lake began to ripple in the breeze. The geese remained, ripping angrily at the grass and clacking their yellowish bills. Unsatisfied, they honked at Lisa, as if it were her fault that the grass was so meager, and lifted themselves into the air.

"*Ay,*" Lisa chirped as she stepped back, frightened by their beating wings. She watched the geese until they, too, disappeared, lost somewhere between the pale stars that had emerged.

Lisa returned inside to do her chores: vacuum, mop, fold laundry, and wash the breakfast dishes in the sink.

When her mother suddenly pulled open the door, Lisa was ironing a pair of her father's pants. She jumped. "You scared me," Lisa said, a hand on her heart. "Who brought you home?"

Her mother ignored Lisa's question and announced breathlessly, "I got me one." She held up a card. For a moment Lisa imagined that her mother had become a citizen, but it was a library card that her mother flashed at her. Tucked under her arm were three books in Spanish: a novel and two books about flowers.

"Estoy orgulloso de ti, Mami. I'm proud of you," Lisa said. She opened one of the books on flowers. It was full of color and Lisa sniffed for a scent. "Mom, I'm surprised!" After all, her mother was shy in public places. She would enter the post office with her head bowed or push Lisa in front of her as they entered a medical clinic. When her mother had to make a call, Lisa dialed and spoke to the person on the other end. Now her first library card! Wasn't that a good first step toward becoming a citizen? Lisa was proud of her mother's big adventure to the library.

After dinner Lisa positioned herself at the kitchen table. She had placed her colored pencils in a coffee cup and opened her sketch pad. Her drawing of the scene in her yard was in lead pencil, but she only had to close her eyes to reassemble it into a magical moment full of vivid colors. She spent an hour on the drawing, looking up now and then at her parents, who had settled in front of the television. Lisa felt tenderness for them. In her mother's lap was one of the library books about flowers, and in her father's hand an English grammar book—both, she realized, were looking to the future.

They want something better, Lisa told herself. They want to move away from this trailer. Cold wind whispered through the cracks, gutters dripped with the last of the rain, Pecas bumped somewhere under the trailer, and the floor seemed to lurch like a ship. Were they on a wide dusty sea in the middle of nowhere? Lisa knew that if she went outside onto the small porch, the night would be black, a color she seldom used in her drawings because she had enough of it in life.

Still, the trailer was home, a home shared by her family and Pecas, a dog she would hug like a pillow because she loved him so much.

The next day at school, Lisa showed Mrs. Mann, her English teacher, the completed drawing. Lisa had imagined that her teacher would assess her deft execution, and, perhaps, be left with a sense of happiness and good fortune—what else was a rainbow over a body of water but something cheerful? And the egrets? Her teacher would coo pleasant words, and Lisa would say, "Yes, aren't they beautiful—and right in my yard! Plus the geese and the calf—all of them."

"Nice," Mrs. Mann concluded after a brief moment. "Is it symbolic? I like what you did with the light."

Symbolic? Lisa wondered. *What does she mean by that?*

The teacher asked, "Does the drawing stand for something? Does it have another meaning?"

"No, it's realistic. You know it rained yesterday? It didn't seem to rain a lot here at school, but there was like a lake by my house." *My house?* Lisa thought. *I mean, my trailer.*

"Yes, it did rain," the teacher remarked absently.

Lisa wasn't sure how to respond, except with the truth. "That's what I saw in my yard. See those birds? Those are egrets. I have an Audubon book, and they're in it." She pointed to the geese. "They're called snow geese. They make a lot of noise when they fly away."

Mrs. Mann nodded and handed the drawing back to Lisa, who could tell that her teacher didn't believe her. Mrs. Mann walked away to put an end to a commotion caused by two boys who were shoving each other.

The bell rang for fourth period. Students slowly found their seats. Lisa was at first confused, then hurt, by the time Mrs. Mann began to interpret a Robert Frost poem about walking in snow. Why didn't her teacher believe what she'd seen?

In fifth-period math Lisa shared her drawing with Guadalupe Reyes, a friend whose father also worked at the dairy. "Where is this?" Guadalupe asked. Her breath smelled of chocolate.

"My house." Lisa spied a candy wrapper tucked in the sleeve of her friend's sweater.

Guadalupe knew Lisa's trailer house and the bare patch of earth where it stood. She knew the rusty tractors, the piles of tires, lumber, scraps of aluminum, the skinny chickens, the makeshift clothesline, the garbage pile, the desolation.

"Your house?" she asked. "It looks different, so pretty." Guadalupe winced at her thoughtless remark, and offered, "Oh, what a dumb thing to say. I'm so sorry."

After school, while hordes waited for the school buses, Lisa appraised her drawing. She didn't mind when someone critiqued her artwork. She anticipated it, longed for it. But this time she was hurt. The scene in the drawing was real. True, she lived in a trailer in the middle of nowhere, but beauty could happen anywhere. She only had to think of the thrush that lived in a junkyard off Highway 99. The thrush was beautiful in spite of its habitat. It only had to chirp its two-note song to convince anyone that it belonged in the world.

The bus ride became rowdy when a boy stole Gaby Lopez's cap and tossed it to another boy. Girls and boys began to shout and tease. Back and forth the cap went until someone tossed it out the window.

"That's mean!" Gaby Lopez screamed. She turned and hollered, "Mr. Baker! It's going to be all dirty."

The bus driver, who seemed to pull back the steering wheel like the horns of a bull, forced the bus to come to a halt. He raised his eyes to the rearview mirror, his eyebrows like hairy tarantulas. "Who did that? Every day it's like this!"

The boys—five of them smirking—looked at their feet. No one answered.

"Who did it?" The driver, breathing hard, unbuckled his seat belt, hitched up his pants as he rose, and walked down the narrow aisle.

"I'll get it, Mr. Baker," Lisa volunteered as she rose from her seat. "I'm just right there." Her trailer house was fifty feet up the road.

"Who did it?" Mr. Baker roared, the tarantulas bristling on his face.

Lisa squeezed around the bus driver to the front door, and descended the steps. She retrieved the hat from the mud and handed it back to Gaby through the open window. "See you tomorrow!" Gaby screamed, her voice happy. Lisa wondered whether Gaby, who was applying lip gloss, liked the boy who had tossed her cap from the bus window. She could imagine them secretly holding hands on a bus ride home.

The bus pulled away, coughing black smoke that made Lisa cover her face with the sleeve of her jacket and mutter a muffled, "*Fuchi*. Stinky."

She started down the road, thinking of the chores and homework she had to do, but she turned when she heard the *caw-caw* of a blackbird and, in the corner of her eye, spotted the calf. It was in the far field, staring at her.

"Cow," she moaned. "Poor cow."

Lisa raced into the field, the mud sucking at her shoes, and thought of how her mother had to trudge in the fields. The earth, Lisa realized, was heavier than she'd thought.

"Don't go," Lisa urged in a low voice as she approached the calf, whose hooves were as muddy as her shoes. "Please don't go."

The calf swung its body around, as if it had heard her plea. It seemed to want to stay.

Lisa slowly trudged through the muddy field, disgusted by the earthy slop stuck to her shoes. *Poor thing,* she thought. *Poor, poor thing. You have nowhere to go. They'll take you back and you'll have to live in dirty straw.*

Lisa envisioned the dairy where her father worked. There were hundreds of cows and calves there. She wondered if they did head counts of the cows at the end of the day. Would they know that one was missing?

The calf remained calm when Lisa began wiping mud from its face and yuck from its small eyes. "I wish I could take you home," she whispered to the calf. "You want to come home with me, huh? We have carrots. You like carrots?" She considered hiding the calf between the rusty tractors, but what kind of life would that be?

She petted the calf, muttered, "I drew you." Her drawing of the scene that occurred in her yard was in her backpack. She could envision it—it was real, it had happened. Lisa realized she had tears on her face. She petted the calf and turned away, no longer mad when the mud sucked her left shoe from her foot. She just whacked the mud from the shoe and fit it back onto her foot.

"I'm going to have to stay here," she uttered. Her parents were old. Their skin was leathery from work, their brows pleated from years of sunlight. Would she have to stay with them in a trailer when they were *really* old? And on this little *rancho,* which was just a patch of forgotten land?

When she returned to her trailer, the lake of water had disappeared. Only a puddle the shape of Florida remained. On that puddle floated an oily rainbow. Lisa tossed her backpack onto the porch and ruffled Pecas's scruff. *How did the lake disappear in one day?* she wondered. *Was the earth that thirsty? Is there a hole below the yard? Maybe I didn't really see it. Maybe it was all made up, like what I see when I draw and paint.*

Lisa pounded her muddy shoe against the railing of the porch. She cursed the wet landing that made her socks wet. She scanned her yard: The lake was gone, really gone. What right did a pair of egrets have to settle in her yard briefly, tease her with beauty and hope, and then fly away?

Identity Theft

THE DAY AFTER Valentine's Day Ana Hernandez arrived at school early intending to sort through her batch of cards. They read be mine, you're the most, sweetie, cutie-pie. If only they were true. No one had ever said, "Be mine," or called her "cutie-pie," an expression from her grandmother's generation. These days, the bolder sixth-grade boys would scream, "You like me, huh?" Still, Ana felt popular as she sorted through her cards, her mouth sweetened by the cinnamon candy a boy had dropped into one of the envelopes. She suspected it was from Peter, but she couldn't be sure.

She was still reading her valentines when her teacher entered the classroom with a new girl. The teacher's smile made Ana curious—was it possible that Ms.

Welty had received a valentine's card from another teacher? There were rumors that she and Mr. Saks, the third-grade teacher, liked each other.

"Ana," Ms. Welty called. "Ana, I want you to meet . . ." The teacher stalled, then smiled, a little color flushing her cheeks. "I want you to meet Ana Hernandez."

Confused, Ana put down a large valentine.

"What I mean," Ms. Welty started to explain, "is that *this* is Ana Hernandez. You two have the same name!"

The original Ana Hernandez glared at the imitation Ana Hernandez. She didn't like it: someone else with *her* name. Also, she had to admit that the *other* Ana Hernandez was pretty, an inch or two taller, and nicely dressed. And was that a cell phone tucked in the pocket of her Tommy Hilfiger jeans? And were those *real* Steve Madden shoes?

But the original Ana quickly replaced the glare in her eyes with something like indifference.

"You got so many valentines," the new Ana sang. She picked one up and sniffed it, her pretty little nose wrinkling in a cute way.

Dang, even her voice is nicer than mine, the original Ana thought spitefully. "These are some of them," she explained. "Most of them I had to carry home in a sack yesterday." She wished she could bite her tongue off and let it crawl away like a snake. That was such an obvious lie!

The new Ana smiled, and the original Ana wondered, *Is she laughing at me?*

It was a weird experience, like looking at a twin sister you had never seen before. The original Ana Hernandez pondered her ill will toward this new girl, and felt that she was being unfair. *She can't help it,* Ana figured, *that she has my name.*

The new Ana fit right into school life. She volunteered to be a crossing guard and helped raise the flag. She helped at a fund-raising car wash and was rumored to have played her flute at an assisted living complex across the street from school. Within a week she was chosen to say the Pledge of Allegiance on the intercom, a special honor usually assigned to students with good grades. She recited it so well that she was assigned to read the school bulletin, which always started with the menu for the day.

The original Ana steamed. She had recited the Pledge of Allegiance on the intercom before, but she had never been asked to read the bulletin. Boldly she approached the principal in the hallway outside the office.

"Mr. Ortiz," she asked, "when can I read the bulletin?"

"But you just did," he countered in surprise.

They soon discovered the error. The reader was supposed to have been the original Ana, not the new Ana. The secretary, they guessed, had made a mistake. When Mr. Ortiz offered the original Ana the chance to read the school bulletin, she grabbed the opportunity. But she felt slighted, and the bulletin she read to the entire school was unimportant. She reported two missing basketballs and a restroom that was going to be closed for the week.

Original Ana observed that new Ana received lots of attention. Ms. Welty would call, "Okay, who can remember when President Lincoln—" and before the teacher could finish her sentence, new Ana would fling her arm up, bracelets jangling. The new Ana didn't do this *all* the time, only at moments when the original Ana knew the answers.

One day when soccer teams were chosen during recess, Becky Ramirez, the star athlete of the school, said, "I'll take Ana Hernandez." The original Ana stepped forward, and Becky snapped, "No, not you—the other Ana. The new girl!" That day Ana was chosen last, and on the field the ball was never passed to her.

In a classroom spelling bee the original Ana had to sit down almost immediately, after she stumbled on *rhinoceros.* The spelling bee became hotly contested between the new Ana and Peter, the boy the original Ana had hoped sent her a special valentine.

"Spell *triangular*," Ms. Welty called to Peter.

He spelled it, wincing as he struggled to get the letters in the proper order. He clenched his fists in victory when Ms. Welty said, "That's correct." In turn, the new Ana eased through the word *magnetic.*

The battle lasted ten minutes. The boys rooted for Peter, and the girls screamed their heads off for the new Ana. In the end Peter prevailed, but the new Ana clapped for the victor and even held up his hand like a champ.

This made the original Ana mad. *She, the newcomer, a fraud, a mere imitation—how dare she touch the hand that put the cinnamon candy in my valentine card!* Ana fumed.

Ana confided in her mother while they were in the kitchen peeling potatoes at the sink. Two onions that would bring tears to their eyes sat on the counter. The daughter was ready for tears, even if they were forced to her eyes by big bloated onions.

"There's nothing wrong," her mother argued softly. Her lined brow expressed her concern for her daughter. "When I was at school, there was another Beatriz Mendoza."

Mendoza was her mother's maiden name, and Beatriz her childhood name. Now she was known as Betty, though some of her friends called her Lu-Lu. Why, Ana could never figure out, but it was a name that her mother responded to.

The original Ana considered being called "Annie." She then thought about using her middle name, Maria. But there were two Marias in the other sixth-grade class, and a third, Ana felt, would be one too many. She then decided, "I'll change my name," and considered Michelle, a pretty name, one that sounded French.

"Michelle Hernandez," she said to her mirror. "My name is Michelle." She giggled and then remembered that her grandmother had a Chihuahua named Michelle, a frighteningly ugly dog with bulging eyes and crooked teeth.

In class Ms. Welty would call, "Ana," and both girls would answer yes. Most times Ms. Welty was seeking out the new Ana.

Then the original Ana concluded, "I shouldn't be stuck-up. I should be friends with her." But by the time the original Ana decided to warm up to the new Ana, she discovered that the newcomer was so popular that they couldn't hang. She just couldn't manage to establish a friendship with the new Ana, even when the original Ana confided, "You know, I have a birthmark on my thigh."

Then a new fad—jangling bracelets first worn by the new Ana—spread throughout the school. "I don't want to wear them," the original Ana fumed, but in the end she, too, wore bracelets and was not above jangling them for no reason except to show she was one of the crowd.

As spring advanced, bringing flowers and freshness to the air, the original Ana drifted away from her classmates. She spent time alone, eating her sandwich, potato chips, and cookies by herself. She began to revel in this quiet time, though occasionally she would look up and see the new Ana at the center of activity. There she was playing four-square or soccer, and escorting guests around school. She was responsible for starting a school garden—tomato and eggplant seeds were first planted in egg cartons. After they'd sprouted, mothers and fathers came to dig up the soil on a Saturday morning. That day the original Ana saw a television crew approaching the new girl.

"Now she's going to be on TV," the original Ana cried.

She was. The new Ana was given ten seconds on

camera. She posed with Peter near the garden, display-
ing an egg carton of tomato plants.

And what could the original Ana do but watch the
new Ana play her flute during a talent show? She had
to swallow her jealousy—yes, that was it—when Peter
joined her to sing a song in French!

The original Ana felt like the Invisible Girl. She
would walk around school, and no one seemed to see
her. One day in the girls' room, she looked at the mirror over the sink, and her reflection was not there.

The mirror was gone, its broken shards gathered up
in a dustpan and thrown away, but the symbolism was
clear.

"She's stolen my identity," the original Ana la-
mented after reading an article in the newspaper about
criminals stealing information about another person.
She chewed a fingernail. Could this *really* happen to
her? She was only twelve, but perhaps years from now
when she got her first credit card, this new Ana would
steal it. Or maybe this new Ana would get in a car wreck
and say *she* had been at fault. Then she swallowed from
fear. She imagined having a baby that was claimed by
the new Ana!

That night she hardly slept. She listened to a dog
overturn the garbage can—or was it the new Ana dig-

ging through the trash, gathering information about their family? She peered outside but saw no one.

During spring break the original Ana learned that her family would be moving. Her father and mother had spoken many times about a new house and often went to open houses on the weekend. Now it was really going to happen—and soon. Her father had gotten a promotion at work and they were moving to Escondido, thirty miles north of their house in Chula Vista.

"The new place has a pool," her father said.

A pool! Ana pictured herself diving into the water and fetching a dime on the bottom. She pictured having friends over for a swim party. *I'll be the new girl!* she thought. *I can make a fresh start, and that Ana can have my stupid old school.*

"It's going to be nice," she mumbled in bed at night, and wondered about the stick-on stars on her ceiling. They'll have to stay, she assumed, and the girl who lives in my bedroom will have something to look at at night.

On the first day at her new school Ana was nervous. *Will they like me?* she wondered. She dressed in her new clothes, and pocketed a cell phone, her first, which she habitually opened and closed.

Her mother escorted her to the office, where Ana

was introduced to a counselor, a woman with a face like a pretty flower and who smelled like a flower when she extended her hand. Two girls, office helpers, said hi. A boy, seated in a chair and with a bloodied elbow—he was still hugging his skateboard—managed to put a smile on his face.

It's nice here, Ana told herself as the counselor led her from the office. Ana could see that the school was clean and modern. The flower beds were flush with yellow and red flowers, and a custodian was mopping up a spill in the hallway.

"Here she is, Ms. Carroll," the counselor announced lightly.

Ana's new teacher approached. Ana liked her right away, and liked how she took her hand in hers.

"I hear you're a very good reader," Ms. Carroll encouraged.

"I guess," Ana answered simply.

Together they entered the classroom, Ms. Carroll prodding her gently. Another girl was hunkered down at her desk, holding a pair of large scissors. *What is she cutting?* Ana wondered, then surmised that she was making a collage.

Ms. Carroll said to the girl, "Ana, I want to you to meet . . ." She stalled, uncertain how to continue. Then she said it: "I want you to meet Ana Hernandez, our new student. Funny, you both have the same name."

The girl glared at Ana, and her scissors chopped at the air. That day, the original Ana became the new Ana. The *new* new Ana couldn't help but falsely praise, "What a nice collage." She brought her hand to her hair and the bracelets on her wrists jangled. The students entering the classroom asked, "Who's she? What's her name?"

"Me?" She turned around in a neat pirouette. "I'm Ana Hernandez."

You Decide

FROM HIS BEDROOM, thirteen-year-old Hector Bustos could hear his parents' voices. They echoed like voices coming down a concrete hallway at a baseball stadium, at a hospital, or the back entrance of a hotel, where bundled trash is tossed into a Dumpster. You open the door, hear freeway noises, and toss.

They were discussing *him*. He could make out his name, but they might as well have been saying "toast" or "bobby pin" or "Doritos." There was not much passion, or nerve, or anything like a tug-of-war. He could never remember them fighting. For years, there had just been a lot of sighing over a toilet seat not put down, or a hand closing like a stone at the kitchen sink when one of them discovered a poorly washed fork. And the laundry? Why did he always hang his shirts so sloppily on the line? And their Lexus? Didn't she know not to park next to a Ford Taurus sure to ding their door?

Hector heard a coffee cup setting back into the saucer. That's how his parents were, nice and tidy, with no rings on their maple furniture. The flowers in the vase were artificial, and the "Great Writers" leather-bound books on the shelf had never been opened. There was an ormolu clock on the mantel, but a spring inside had broken.

"Hector," he heard his mom calling. She called a second time, and her voice grew slightly angry: "Hector, we want to talk with you."

He had already concluded that it involved their divorce. All of his friends' parents were divorced or divorcing. It was nothing new.

"Coming!" he shouted. He breathed in deeply, blew out a lungful of air, opened the door of his bedroom, and walked down the hallway into the living room.

They were there, looking neither happy nor unhappy. It was something in between, like when you get in your car and just drive, your eyes lifting to see in the rearview mirror where you've been.

That's what he was thinking. They get in their car and drive a lot—to work, to the store, to a pastry shop to put sweets in their mouths, to places where he imagined they sat and looked straight ahead. They would look into the rearview mirror now and then and see nothing but blackness.

"Yeah," he said. He stood like a penguin, his arms like useless wings at his sides.

His parents' mouths retracted into small puckers. Neither liked the word *yeah*, but they contained their displeasure. They had more important things to say.

"Hector," his mother started, then paused.

Hector noticed her smoothing her lap, as if she were inviting him to come and sit. But the last time he had climbed into her lap—he was five, he remembered, and he was holding a baby tooth that had just fallen out— she had told him to get down, that he was big enough to sit in a chair. He did as he was told. From across the living room, he'd held up the tooth and said, "See?"

"Hector," his father began. His face was moist with something that was not tears. *What is it?* Hector wondered. *Worry?*

"Hector," his mother repeated. "You decide."

Hector had been prepared by Trent Johnson, a friend at school. Trent's parents were divorced and he'd had to decide who he wanted to live with. Trent had decided to live with his father, who had promised him a bow-and-arrow set. He would get a car when he turned seventeen.

"Yeah, I know," remarked Hector, the new taste of bitterness in his mouth.

At the use of the word *yeah,* his mother winced and crumpled the Kleenex in her grip. It looked like a white carnation.

"What do you mean you know?" his father asked. His tie was loosened, but he still seemed choked by work.

"I just know. You want me to decide who I should live with."

"So you know everything," his mother nearly snapped. She crushed the Kleenex again.

"I didn't say that," Hector risked arguing and added snidely, "I'm only getting Bs." He was surprised how that came out. Was he getting braver?

His father sighed, leaned forward, and palms out, said that they both loved him. Hector had to be mature and decide who he would like to live with. Would an hour be long enough?

"Yes," Hector answered this time.

He returned to his bedroom, where he sat on his bed, a little mousy squeak coming from the springs. He pressed a flashlight against his palm: blood bright, blood dark, blood bright, blood dark. It was a signal to someone far away, a beacon to commandos to land and retake the shore. But he stopped the flashlight game and took a drink of his soda, a hardy gulp that burned his throat and misted his eyes.

"I don't want to be with either of them," he muttered. He looked up at the poster of Alex Smith, quarterback for the 49ers, once a great team but now full of players who fell over like bowling pins. Still, he wished Alex Smith were more than a picture on a poster, wished he could say, "Hector, meet me out back."

Hector had the urge to crawl out his bedroom window into the evening's darkness. The urge became real when he unlatched the screen and backed out, feet first, wiggling for the touch of ground. He scraped his elbow when he leaped to the lawn, as soft as a grave. He dabbed spit on his scrape and moved quickly away from the safety light that had come on.

Alex Smith wasn't waiting in the yard with a squirt bottle in his hand asking, "Thirsty?" There was no one, just a small plum tree tossing its head back and forth in the autumn breeze. Hector had helped plant the tree the year before and was scolded because his shovel had grazed the ball of roots. His father complained under his breath that the tree was now ruined, and if it didn't have plums in two years, they would know why.

Hector left by the side gate and hurried away, thankful that the neighbor's dog didn't bark, that his parents were in the living room looking straight ahead or maybe at the floor, the shag rug crushed underfoot.

He jogged for a block and then slowed to a walk. The houses, Hector realized, stayed after a family split up. True, the lawns browned for a while, but there was always fertilizer to bring them back. Flowers could be plugged into the ground and new families would applaud the colors. The sound of the water features outside could hide the screaming inside.

And who ventured out for Halloween? Hector had dressed up as Batman for two years and every time he flew up the steps of a house, porch lights turned off. He could see the flicker of televisions and people ghosting about in their bathrobes. But they wouldn't answer the door. One woman had opened her mail slot and passed him a packet of chewing gum, but she was the only one. No one is nice here, Hector brooded after that experience. You can fall off your bike, and your neighbor turns the other way.

Hector thought of his uncle Rudy, a cowboy type, rough from banging tumbleweeds out of his way, wrestling steer, bucking hay, and spitting into the wind. He didn't think twice about dropping a hatchet on a chicken's neck or about bats hanging in the barn, their eyes red as coals. He hissed at rattlesnakes, hammered fences into the earth, and stared down coyotes that raised their lean heads from the arroyo. He'd told Hector that once, when he couldn't find a razor, he broke a beer bottle and used it to shave his stubble.

Hector wondered how far he had to walk to get to Uncle Rudy's place across town and beyond the railroad tracks. Where he lived was kind of like the Wild West—neighbors yelling, dogs and roosters fighting, radios screaming, mud and mosquitoes everywhere, and the moon always orange and hanging over them. Kids with rickets ate oatmeal morning, noon, and night.

"I want to live with you," he muttered under his breath. He spat. That's what his uncle would have done if he'd been told, "You decide." He should have spat right on the rug, and maybe released a bigger one on the plasma TV.

It seemed to Hector that the orange moon, muscling itself into the tainted sky, was a good sign. That would be his big flashlight, his beacon, his shiny path sparkling with glass. His uncle would be sitting on his back steps, his boots off. Who cared if his socks didn't match or were full of holes or if they smelled mightier than the skunks that came to visit?

"I'm going there," Hector moaned. "I'll live with Uncle." He pictured himself opening a can of spaghetti and eating right out of the can. So what if it was cold? So what if he ate that slop with a knife? He would sleep on the floor and read westerns in which the heroes used barbed wire to floss their teeth. Their combs for their dusty pompadour hairstyles? Big old pitchforks.

He was debating how to find Uncle (follow the banged-up moon to the poor part of town?) when out of the shadows appeared a ragged dog the color of dirty water. Leaves were hooked in his fur. His left ear was nearly gone, one eye was half closed, and fur was missing around his neck. The dog was a refugee, but from where? He had certainly known fights in his time.

"Hey, pooch," Hector greeted and snapped his fingers.

But the dog didn't have time for Hector. He began limping down the street, his eyes shifty in his small head, determined to get somewhere.

"You know where you're going, huh?" Hector sang as he trailed the dog, whose nails clicked on the asphalt. He was determined to keep up with the dog; whether he got to his uncle's place became unimportant. He just felt the urge to journey with a dog that frolicked, fought, and tramped through his years.

A year ago, they had a dalmatian, which had always made Hector think of illness. The dog was quiet. His nose was dry as a leaf. When you showed him his bowl of water, he whimpered. When you petted him, fur came off in your palm. They got rid of the dog when his mother bought new living room furniture.

Hector tagged along, and the dog hurried, scared not by Hector but by something from the east—the coming night when the bats would unlatch themselves and circle the hairdos of pretty girls? The dog was rushing away from badness, or toward goodness, following some dog philosophy of survival.

Hector began to think that the dog had fallen out of the back of a truck and that his instincts were telling him, *Go this way. This way is home.* His own instincts told him to lick a finger and hold it up. *Go where the wind blows, where all the debris gathers along a fence,* he told himself. *Cows will bellow beyond the fence and become your friends.*

The dog suddenly stopped to drink from a puddle. He rolled his purplish tongue over his chops. He sniffed the wind, let his stream flow down the trunk of a tree, and chewed at a flea in his fur. Finished with his doggy business, he began to trot, with Hector in tow.

But three blocks later, Hector paused when he heard

a voice call, "Yoo-hoo." An elderly woman was in her driveway, a small stool at her side, in the near dark.

"Me?" Hector replied, pointing a finger like a gun at his heart. He ran over to her.

The woman had locked her keys in her car and had been trying to work a coat hanger inside the window to lift the knob of the lock. She would try, fail, sit down on her stool, weep because no one would help, and try again. She had been at it for nearly an hour.

"Silly me," she chimed, lowering herself onto her three-legged stool and smoothing her lap in a motherly way. Her face was overly painted, her teeth red from lipstick. Clouds of perfume rose from the folds in her neck. She dabbed her brow with a handkerchief and whimpered, "Poor me, silly me."

"Nah, ma'am, it happens all the time," argued Hector. "It really does."

Hector was schooled on what to do with a coat hanger. Uncle Rudy had taught him. It was something, Uncle Rudy had argued, that every man—and woman—needed to master. The old bird of an uncle had also taught Hector to hot-wire a car and siphon gas.

"My son lives in Turlock," the woman said absently. She confessed that he didn't have time for her, that he was a fertilizer salesman always on the road.

Hector noticed that her own lawn was brownish. *Couldn't her son come by and sprinkle pellets on her lawn?* he wondered. Then an awful thought struck him. Was he going to be like her son, on the road forever? Would he be a fertilizer salesman throwing pellets on every lawn except his mother's? The image evaporated as he realized this elderly woman smelled like a flower too close to his face, and that his mother—he winced—gave off a scent of ink. She was a part-time Realtor, and what mattered to her was when the ink dried—or so he remembered her saying on the phone.

"There," he said, and opened the car door so he could pull the keys from the ignition.

The woman applauded as she rose from the stool—an ovation for his handiwork. She gave him a pale five-dollar bill, which Hector thought must have gone through the wash. It was soft, clean, and faded, perhaps bleached in a load of whites. Any other time, Hector would have declined the money, but he remembered his uncle, who, if he had appeared from behind that ancient car, would have scolded, "Boy, don't be stupid! Take that money!" It was five dollars for the road.

After this untimely chore, Hector turned, full of panic, because the dog was gone. He called, "Dog, dog, where are you?" He sprinted down the street and found the canine poking his nose into a McDonald's bag. His whiskered face rose from the bag; a French fry hung like a cigarette from his mouth.

The two continued their journey.

Hector followed behind, then moved in front when the dog stopped to sniff a lawn, and finally ended up at his side. They were companions, or so Hector wanted to believe. They were leaving the subdivision, saying *adiós*. His parents—Hector could envision them— would be sitting on the couch, looking straight ahead. Now and then they would look at the clock. Was the hour over yet?

Leaves scuttled in the wind. Trees shook, overwatered lawns leaked, and porch lights seemed to turn off as they passed. When he asked, "It's not far, is it?" the dog, still in full trot, raised his ruined eyes to Hector. Life, Hector figured, is going to send you to mysterious places.

"I'm going to find a real family," he told himself. He was going to a better place, somewhere where he could live with nature, run with dogs, and howl at the moon.

The Babysitter

"I DON'T WANT YOU TWO to goof off," Rachael's mother warned. She was applying lipstick, and lots of it. She made a face at the mirror, as if the heavy application were the reflection's fault. She dabbed her lips and turned to her children. "You hear me?"

"Yeah, we won't mess up," Rachael agreed. She figured that she and Freddie had already messed up earlier in the day when they'd been jumping from their neighbor's plum tree. They returned home with bloody elbows. Freddie's lip was swollen and a baby tooth had become as wobbly as a restaurant chair.

Their parents were divorced, but neither of the kids missed a father who sent them presents and money only now and then. Life was like the game of jumping from trees: Sometimes it was fun, and sometimes you got to your feet crying.

The kids watched their mother put on earrings. They were excited for her—a girlfriend was picking her up and they were going to a dance. Rachael and Freddie were going to get a babysitter they'd never met; they hoped she would be fun. They had a rented movie to watch, and their mother had bought them a frozen pizza as large as a sombrero.

"You look pretty, Mom," Freddie said.

"You smell pretty, too," Rachael added. She was about to compliment her on how her dress matched her shoes when the doorbell rang.

The kids jumped and screamed, "It's her!" "Her" was a girl recommended by her mom's *comadre* Lucy. The babysitter had dropped out of school at seventeen, Lucy had said, but she was a good kid and needed work.

When Rachael opened the door, she was surprised to find a girl whose nose was spiked with two chrome rings. She had dark liner under her eyes, and her hair was orange. Studs adorned her ears, six at Rachael's quick count. Her fishnet stockings were pulled awkwardly over her pale thighs.

"Are you the babysitter?" Rachael asked, slightly frightened.

"Yeah," the girl answered flatly. She entered the house, her big boots ringing against the floor. Her long black coat dragged like a shadow.

Girls aren't supposed to be dressed like that, Rachael found herself thinking, noticing that the coat covered a dress that was too, too short. Her fingernails were painted black. And was that a tattoo circling her wrist?

When her mother clip-clopped into the living room to meet the babysitter, Rachael could see that she was transfixed for a long second before she snapped out of it and said, "You must be Keri."

"Yeah," the girl answered. That one word revealed a chrome ball on her tongue.

"What's that?" Freddie asked, pointing.

"What's what?" his mother peered down at him.

"In her mouth?" Freddie's own tongue appeared, then quickly retracted as if someone might staple a chrome ball to it.

Embarrassed, Rachael squeezed her eyes shut and wished the babysitter's arrival could begin again. Her little brother was such a punk! Rachael expected her mother to admonish Freddie, but she only sighed and looked at her watch. She set rules: one movie, the pizza for dinner, no answering the front door, and no use of the telephone. If they played the stereo, they shouldn't turn it on too loudly.

Soon she was out the door, with a kissy peck for Rachael and two gentle kisses on Freddie's cheek—his lip was still tender. To Keri, she offered a reminder that she should call if there was trouble.

After the front door closed, Keri sat at the kitchen table, her chin in the palm of her hand. Rachael attempted to liven things up. She showed Keri the scrapes on her elbows and recounted how these injuries had occurred. But this display didn't move Keri. Rachael pondered. She decided to inform this babysitter that they were excellent students. Rachael told Keri that she was ten and that her little brother was seven, but they could—and did—already read novels. She described a book about a boy whose parents had moved away without telling him. Rachael chuckled as she recounted a scene of the boy washing the dog in the bathtub.

Keri yawned and revealed a second chrome knob in her mouth.

Rachael then foolishly asked, "What grade are you in?"

"Grade, like, you mean, school?" Keri's eyes were flat. "I'm, like, outta school." She bit a fingernail.

"I'm in second," Freddie said. He then displayed his scraped elbows and showed Keri his thumb, which a fishing hook had punctured when he was real little.

"I'm bored," Keri announced as she brought out a cigarette from the inside of her shirt pocket.

"You smoke?" Rachael asked.

Keri lit up and blew a perfect halo of smoke that hung in the air for a few seconds before it broke apart.

"Smoking's bad," Freddie claimed. "I burned my fingers once."

Keri inhaled and held the smoke in her lungs. Then she slowly let it unfurl and take shape in the air; for a second it resembled a dragon with a whipping tail. But like the halo, it, too, broke apart. She rose and went to the refrigerator.

"What do you got to eat?"

"Pizza!" Freddie screamed.

"Mom also rented us a movie," said Rachael, who was a little put off by this girl. She was unfriendly and just too weird. Rachael surmised that was why she had dropped out: no friends to hang out with. Who would wear a big black coat when it's not cold or raining? And all those metal things in her face? They reminded Rachael of her dad's fishing tackle.

Keri brought the pizza out of the freezer. With a fork, she stabbed at the plastic that encased the pizza while the cigarette hung from her mouth. The ash grew and the cap of red brightened each time she stabbed and struggled with the plastic wrapping. Finally, she fit the pizza into the microwave, but discovered that it was too large—she had to bend it slightly.

Rachael watched as Keri punched in the time and inhaled on her diminishing cigarette. Not wishing to get caught in the stinky smoke, Rachael scooted out of the kitchen and into the living room. Freddie had slid in the DVD and was sitting inches from the screen. He turned and announced, "It's *Nemo*."

Rachael could feel her mouth tighten. How many times had they seen that babyish movie? Rachael was suddenly aware that Keri was a lot older, especially in experience. Why else would she have a tattoo circling her wrist and one on the back of her neck? Rachael had spied them when Keri had pulled back her hair. Didn't that mean maturity?

Keri appeared in the living room. "What are you going to watch?" she asked.

"*Nemo!*" Freddie screamed.

"Whatever." Keri plopped on the couch and opened

her cell phone. No messages. She slunk into the couch, eyes closed, her legs splayed. She scratched her orange hair and breathed deeply.

She thinks we're babies, Rachael realized as she sat a few feet behind her brother on the floor. *I don't care. She stinks of smoke.*

The movie drowned out the hum of the microwave. They watched *Nemo,* and Rachael found herself pulled into the narrative. She was startled by a loud pop.

They all jumped up, even Keri, who had fit a grape -flavored lollipop into the corner of her mouth. They scampered into the kitchen, where the window of the microwave was lit more dramatically than the TV screen.

"Oh, my God," Rachael let out.

The microwave beeped. Rachael opened the door slowly. Through the curling steam, the pizza appeared to ooze from the microwave. It reminded Rachael of the movie *The Blob.*

"I guess fifteen minutes was too long," Keri remarked. She tapped the crust and licked her finger. "It's still tasty."

"I'm hungry," Freddie said.

"You can eat the pizza like soup," Keri said seriously. "I could put it in a bowl."

Pizza in a bowl! Rachael grimaced. "How about a sandwich?" she asked. "With all the chips you want."

Freddie rolled his eyes as he judged his sister's recommendation. "No," he concluded. "I want something better."

"How 'bout a hamburger?" Keri suggested.

Freddie's mouth arched into a smile, but he released his show of happiness because his spreading grin disturbed his swollen lip.

"We're going to have to drive," Keri said. "Burger King's far away."

"You have a car?" Rachael inquired, searching for a spatula to scrape the cheese from the walls of the microwave.

"I walked. We can use your mom's car."

Rachael stopped. "My mom's car?" She pictured Keri turning corners at ninety miles an hour. "That's, like, against the rules. Mom will really get mad."

"So are you hungry or not?" Keri bent over, fiddled with her fishnet stockings and pulled her ringing cell phone from her boot. She frowned at the number and coolly ignored the call.

"We'll just have sandwiches," Rachael replied.

Rachael made peanut butter and jelly sandwiches for the three of them, and poured potato chips into a bowl. Keri waved her sandwich away, but pinched up a few potato chips. She pulled a candy bar from her purse and took a bite. She then handed the candy bar to Freddie.

Rachael didn't like Freddie eating candy before his meal, even if it was just a sandwich and potato chips. *She's just awful.* Rachael brooded and bit into her sandwich. She munched dramatically to demonstrate that the sandwich, prepared by her own hands, was a tasty treat. She then crunched on a potato chip hard— the chip broke noisily.

But Rachael slowed her eating when Keri brought a slick chrome projectile from her boot and spanked it against her thigh. She uncapped it and applied the black filmy gloss to her lips.

"Black lip gloss," Rachael commented, disgusted.

"Ugh." Freddie rested his candy wrapper on the coffee table.

"It's just makeup. It's like when you dress up for Halloween." Keri stood up and rifled through her coat pocket until she found an earring. "Here, put this on." She unscrewed the post and said that it would look nice hanging from his nose.

"Don't!" Rachael warned. The idea of her little brother wearing an earring in his nose—or any other part of his body—was too much. Rachael began to wonder if there was a law against babysitters like this one.

Freddie studied the earring. "It's for girls," he concluded.

Keri posted her hands on her hips and barked a single laugh. "Are pirates girls? They wear earrings."

"Not in their noses!" Rachael spoke up.

Freddie seemed to think deeply. "Nah, pirates ain't girls. They got, like, swords and knives."

"Ain't isn't a real word," Rachael corrected with a growl.

"Ain't so!" Keri said, and laughed. "It's a real word. I ain't got a problem with it." She ran a hand through her hair and applied her black lip gloss again.

Rachael became starched with surprise when Freddie fit the earring onto his nose and slowly turned the knob until it stayed. He shook his head, and the earring wiggled.

"How do I look?" he asked.

"Ugly," Rachael answered.

He ran to the bathroom with Keri to apply the black lip gloss.

"Don't!" Rachael scolded as she followed in long strides.

"Relax," Keri said. "We're just having fun. It's better than watching a stupid movie."

Rachel had to admit that it was sort of fun seeing her goofy little brother with an earring hanging from his nose. Still, she had to take a stand. "But it's not normal," Rachael countered.

"What's normal?" Keri stated that there were all sorts of ways to dress. Look at Africa, she argued. People wore bones through their noses and cheeks.

"Yes, that's okay *there*," Rachael argued. "But we're here in America."

"Shallow people in America wear jeans and T-shirts. Get with it."

Rachael was hurt, and it showed in her reddening cheeks. "So it's okay to wear ugly stuff like those stockings of yours? They're cheap!"

"No, they cost quite a bit." Keri gazed at her long legs and adjusted her fishnets.

"Did it hurt?" Freddie butted in.

"Did what hurt?"

"Those things in your face." He pointed.

Keri let out a small barking laugh. "Like, yeah, it hurt." But she contended that she had suffered greater pains in life than what it took to staple her lip, nose, ears, and belly button. She bent over and brought out a small packet from her boot. "Italian coffee—it's the best."

"What's Italian coffee?" Rachael asked.

Keri didn't bother to explain. She went to the kitchen, with Rachael and Freddie following. There she brewed the coffee in a saucepan and strained it into a coffee mug.

"Here," she said, and presented the cup to Rachael, who searched the surface of the hot, steamy brew. She could see her reflection, and suddenly she could see herself with a stud in her nose—something small as dust, something dainty. She then brought the hot coffee to her lips, sipped, and gave her tongue a few seconds to appraise the taste. She then uttered, "Strong."

"You have to get used to it," Keri advised. "If you want, add sugar."

Freddie said, "Let me try." He loaded the coffee cup with sugar and slowly brought it to his lips. He sipped, smacked his lips, and sipped again. "It's good."

Rachael took the cup from Freddie, sipped, and had to admit that its deliciousness agreed with her. *Is this what Goth-types drink?* she wondered. She drained the cup.

"You know what?" Keri said after they drank two

mugs of coffee each. "Rachael, you need to punk out." She went to her coat draped on the couch, brought a small bottle out of her pocket, and shook it. "Let's color your hair."

"No way!" Rachael screamed. She took a step back.

"You can wash it out," Keri argued. "It's not permanent. Come on, be mellow."

"Let me," Freddie begged. His grin revealed what was left of his baby teeth.

"Okay," Keri said. She seemed to weigh the wisdom of coloring the hair of a seven-year-old.

Rachael was amazed when, in the bathroom, Freddie bent his head over the tub and allowed Keri to work the dye into his hair. It lathered into a mountainous, orange frothy concoction.

"Close your eyes tight," Keri warned.

Rachael was worried that Freddie's eyes might turn orange as pumpkins and perhaps grow just as large if they became infected. After all, the dye had been in Keri's boot and there was no telling if maybe some of her foot germs had rubbed off when she opened the bottle. But when his head was toweled off, Freddie fluttered his eyes open. They weren't orange, but his head sure was. Keri then streaked his hair with green gel.

"Cool," Keri crowed as she stepped back to appraise her creation: a seven-year-old punker with scrapes on his elbows!

He's like a parakeet, Rachael thought.

Standing on a stool, Freddie looked in the fogged-up mirror. He wiped the mirror and judged his appearance after he turned his head at different angles.

Keri next attached a row of screw-on earrings to his earlobes. She dabbed a dark substance under his eyes.

"I look like the dudes in the Raiders Black Hole," Freddie said.

Rachael could picture those wild fans at the Oakland Raiders games. They were hideous and dangerous. "You sure it'll come out?" she asked.

"I'm sure," Keri said. "How 'bout you now?"

Rachael stepped back, her hand on the doorway. "No, thank you. I like my hair the way it is."

"Don't be a chicken!" Freddie sneered. "Before Mom comes home, we can wash it out."

"No, I don't think so." She posted her hands on her hips.

But when they returned to the living room and Keri put Spew Face on the stereo, Rachael had to giggle and join in bouncing to the music. It felt fun; it felt wild. At first she just jumped lightly but then picked up speed when she and Freddie leaped on the couch. He began to jump and touch the ceiling.

"Go, boy!" Keri encouraged over the blare of "Ugly Mom, Ugly Sister." They stopped when the song ended, but got up again when the next song, "Dog Breath Friendship," started with a howling dog and a guitar solo. They were punishing the living room, jumping wildly.

But when Freddie leaped from the couch to the hassock to the end table, he slipped on a doily and went headfirst onto the carpeted floor.

"Ahhhh," he cried, hand on top of his head. Between his fingers, blood bubbled and rolled down his wrist.

Rachael's eyes widened. Were her little brother's brains—his one important possession, because she had to admit that he wasn't cute—about to come out? She should have known that dancing in close quarters to a group called Spew Face would bring them to disaster. His hair was now a psychedelic mixture of orange, green, and red.

"You'll be okay," Keri said without emotion.

But Rachael could tell that she, too, was a little nervous. Was he really going to be okay? Freddie was leaping around the living room again, and for a moment

Rachael believed that he was still dancing to the music. But he was leaping from pain, or fear, or both. The earring fell from his nose, and the black under his eyes began to crawl like fingers down his cheeks.

The dance party was over. "Is he going to die?" Rachael asked.

"Of course not!" Keri led Freddie to the bathroom, and started to bathe his head.

"It hurts." Freddie bawled.

"It's not that bad," Keri said. She washed his head gently with a bar of soap and then started to scrub when the dye didn't rinse out. "The orange isn't coming out." She examined the washcloth and could see the green gel, the black from under his eyes, and pinkish blood.

"Mom's going to be really mad," Rachael predicted. "I told you you shouldn't have."

"Well, he wanted it."

"But you said it would come out."

Keri stood up, her chest heaving. "Well, sorry, it doesn't. What's the big deal?"

"What about the cut on his head?" Rachael asked.

"It's no biggie. It's already stopped bleeding."

Rachael parted Freddie's hair and probed the wound with her finger. It was a bloodless slit, which made her wonder whether all the blood in his head was gone. She looked at her brother, who seemed pale as he stood up, a stream of water rushing down his neck. Was he about to faint, or "succumb," a grown-up word she had learned meant to die?

"Are you sure you're okay?" Rachael held Freddie's shoulders. "Do you feel like you're going to . . . succumb?"

"No, I'm not going to throw up," he answered.

Rachael left it at that.

"It just hurts a little," he said, sniffing.

But his tears stopped when Keri brought from her boot a Butterfinger candy bar. She unwrapped part of it, and said, "Here." He bit into it, a flake falling from his lips.

They all went to the living room, where *Finding Nemo* was muted and Spew Face was blaring. When Keri turned off the music, the house became suddenly silent. She bent down and picked up the earring.

"What are we going to tell my mom?" Rachael asked.

Keri shrugged.

They sat watching the final scenes of *Nemo*. When the credits began to roll, Rachael suggested that she and Freddie go to bed. Any other time, Freddie would have fought such a proposal, but he rose without complaint and shuffled off to his bedroom. He didn't bother to say good night.

"What do you think my mom's going to say?" Rachael asked.

"Jeez, I said I'm sorry. What else do you want me to do?" Keri brought a fingernail to her mouth and chewed.

"Sorry might not be good enough."

Keri began to work on another fingernail.

Rachael went into the kitchen, where the exploded pizza still hung from the microwave. She cleaned up the gooey mess, washed the grease-spotted floor, did the few dishes in the sink, and went to brush her teeth.

I'm going to be normal, she promised herself. *I don't care if I wear jeans and T-shirts. And what kind of band has a name like Spew Face?*

Rachael didn't bother to say good night to Keri. She went to her bedroom, dressed in her pajamas, hopped into bed, and closed her eyes. But she couldn't sleep. She thought of her mother on the dance floor. She pictured her mother's earrings swinging on her lobes as she danced to a nice singer like Céline Dion. Rachael tossed and turned, punched her pillow, thought of Keri on the couch eating her fingernails, then recharged the image of her mother on the dance floor. She imagined her mother's earring flying into the air, and she imagined a nice man bending to pick it up.

"Come on—go to sleep," she mumbled. She was tired of the day—let it be over!

Rachael then remembered the coffee she had drunk. It was keeping her awake, she figured, and maybe she would never sleep again!

"Sleep!" she scolded herself as she rolled onto her belly. But Keri's face kept reappearing with more things pierced in her nose, including—would this be possible?—a large lock.

"Sleep, I tell you," she scolded her body.

Rachael turned over in bed, listening to the house creak, and held her breath when she heard the front door open—her mother was home. She got up and quietly opened her bedroom door, listening for voices.

"Was everything okay?" her mother asked.

"Yeah," Keri answered.

"Liar," Rachael whispered, then closed the door. Wait until morning! She imagined Freddie walking into the kitchen with his orange hair—maybe bloody from his reopened wound!

Rachael returned to bed. She still couldn't sleep. The clock on her chest of drawers glowed 12:24. She squeezed her eyes, then relaxed her eyes. She rolled onto her stomach, her back, and her side. Nothing worked to make her fall into a slumber.

"I shouldn't have drunk it," she mumbled. She began to realize what made adults so grumpy: the coffee they threw down their throats every morning. They drank that horrible stuff, and at night they couldn't sleep. They rolled around in bed and revisited the scenes of the day. How many times had her mother told her of insomnia?

Toward dawn Rachael had a dream about flying, and woke with the feeling of anvils on her eyelids. She sat on the edge of her bed, sighed, and slid her feet into her slippers.

"I feel tired," she moaned. She assumed this was how adults woke up every day: tired but hankering for more coffee to straighten them out.

She passed her brother's bedroom and peeked in. There he was, asleep, with his orange hair. She shook her head, closed the door, and decided not to worry.

Her mother was in the kitchen reading the newspaper. Her dark hair (dyed black, Rachael knew) was wild. Her eyes were puffy as if she, too, hadn't slept.

"How did you sleep, little princess?" her mother asked.

"Okay." Rachael sat at the table with her mother. *Soon she'll know,* Rachael thought. *Soon Freddie will appear from his bedroom.* For now she didn't care. No, she wanted to be like her mother.

"Mom." Rachael exhaled.

"What, girl?" her mother asked as she turned the page of the newspaper.

"Mom, I want a cup of coffee."

Although she was only ten, she felt she had become a grown person. She had not slept well and she had a burden she couldn't quite explain. She hoped a dark brew, with cream and sugar, would wake her up.

Citizen of the World

LAURITA MALAGÓN SPUN the globe in the library. As it squeaked on its axis, she closed her eyes and dragged a finger on its glossy surface until the globe slowed to a stop. *This is where I'm from,* she told herself. Her eyes fluttered open. Her finger had stopped near New Zealand and a ring of islands in a vast blue ocean. *Is that where they have coconuts?* she wondered. *Or is it penguins? Or maybe it's the place where they play the ukulele.*

Summer school was reading, drawing, and folk dancing from Texas and Ireland, which were both far away for eleven-year-old Laurita. Summer school was also math, done on a calculator, and singing, which made her cheeks bloom like red poppies.

She wasn't able to dwell long on New Zealand. Her teacher, Mrs. Moore, was calling everyone to hurry up. They were on their weekly visit to the school library to scout for fresh books. Several sixth graders would enter the library at a time, choose a book, and leave as quietly as mice. That was the rule.

New Zealand, Laurita reflected, with enough dreaminess in her heart to make her stride lightly from the library. *That's where I'm really from. I'm from an island so far from any continent that birds can't fly there, or people get there, unless they board a ship or a plane. I'm exotic.*

Exotic.

She had learned this word when a friend described a fruit drink she had drained in twenty seconds in Orlando, Florida. *Exotic* was the flavor of the week. The drink came with a tiny umbrella, as if its ice cubes needed shade; it came with a plump cherry and a sprig of mint. Models in magazines wearing hoop earrings were exotic. A flower with a pinwheel of tropical colors was exotic. A poodle with a ball of fur at the end of its tail was exotic, plus kind of cute.

Laurita knew full well she wasn't from New Zealand. Her father and mother spoke Spanish, and a few phrases in English: "It's really hot." "Oh, doggone it." "That's too much, my friend." Like parrots they could say words—"shoes," "milk," "bed," "bargain"—but couldn't easily connect them into sentences. Her parents, both of whom worked at Big Lots as janitors, remained mostly monolingual.

Monolingual. Laurita had learned that word in second grade. A big person had asked, "Are you bilingual?" To this she playfully shrugged her shoulders. The person then asked, "Are you trilingual?" She added an embarrassed grin to her shrug. Then the person said, "Oh, you must be monolingual."

Laurita had shrugged, grinned, and kicked a toe at the ground. She answered in accented English, "I speak two languages." She unfolded two fingers and held them up.

But she actually knew other languages, too. When her mother served Top Ramen for dinner, Laurita would thank her with what Japanese she knew: *"Arigato."* If she ate a hamburger, which she discovered was a German food, she would peel back the bun and whisper for the fun of it, *"Danke, danke.* Thanks, thanks." And she did like Chinese pork buns; her mother would tease, saying that she was adopted from a princess in the Far East.

Who was she, really?

That day at the library, Laurita checked out the novel *Heidi*. Instead of playing a rowdy game of four-square with her friends, she sucked on Jolly Ranchers and read three chapters of a story set in Switzerland. She kept looking at the cover of the book and dreamily pondered little Heidi. She was pretty, the valley green, the sheep white, and the sky bluer than any color found in her pack of 48 Crayolas.

When she asked her teacher about the word *yodeling*, Mrs. Moore lent her a CD of *The Sound of Music*. Laurita was smitten by the sound of yodeling. She played the song over and over, and then she, too, began to yodel. She yodeled before dinner, yodeled after dinner, and yodeled during dinner until her parents told her politely to knock it off. In the shower, away from the commotion of her family, she yodeled. It was the happiest sound in the world.

On Sunday after church, her father blew the dust off an old 45 record, set it on a phonograph as old as time, and lowered the needle on the first song, "*Canción de Mi Vida.*" Laurita was stirred by the yodeling female singer. *How is it possible,* she thought, *this yodeling in a song in Spanish?* Her father, his hands on his belly, basked in the sounds of the song.

"But, *Papi,* it sounds like it's from Switzerland," she explained to him. She played the song again and, yes, the yodeling was there. Her father explained the German influence on Mexican music. He tapped his toe to the beat.

Laurita yodeled to that Mexican song and yodeled to the flip side. She didn't care when the dog next door began to howl, or that her little brothers, the jokers, also began to howl.

But who was she—really?

"What's happening to the world?" her father remarked sadly. It was a regular Wednesday evening when nothing important had occurred, except that her brothers Miguel Dos and Kirby had gotten bee stings on their toes within seconds of each other.

After work, it was her father's habit to read the local Spanish-language newspaper in the yard. He read about a raid that had deported a family of six. His mustache jumped at the news of the government cracking down on so-called illegals. You could go out to buy milk and find yourself picked up in a van and heading for Tijuana. You could go to return a video and *la migra,* the immigration police, would be outside waiting for you.

"*Viejo,* what will happen if they catch all the people?" Laurita's mother asked as she walked onto the back porch with a pitcher of iced tea.

"*Nada,*" he answered sagely. "We're citizens of the world." He accepted the glass of iced tea with a "*Gracias, vieja.*"

Citizens of the world, Laurita pondered. She liked that phrase. She had felt that way for a long time, ever since she got her own library card with her name on it. And wasn't it true that she had a license plate that read laura attached to the back of her bike seat? She could roll up one side of their driveway and down the other side as long as she pleased. And couldn't she yodel just like singers in Mexico *and* Switzerland?

One day when their parents were working, Laurita's two little brothers rifled through the desk where bills, prescriptions, hand-scrawled recipes, old sepia-colored photographs of relatives in Mexico, pens and pencils bundled in rubber bands, and important documents were kept.

"This is mine!" Miguel Dos exclaimed when he held up his birth certificate.

"This is mine!" Kirby screamed, even prouder. "Look how little my foot was."

Laurita searched that desk, but couldn't locate her birth certificate. This stopped her yodeling, the bird inside her suddenly quieted. Later at the playground, she froze when she saw an official-looking car parked outside the fence. Was it *la migra*? Was it there to round up kids screaming on the monkey bars? Shoo them out from under bushes where they lurked, playing hide-and-seek?

Laurita thought her family might have a better chance with *la migra* if they practiced English. That evening, when the dinner dishes had been removed to the sink to soak, Laurita ordered everyone to stay put. She had a game she wanted them to play, and dashed off to get her dictionary.

The parents looked nervously at each other, not unlike when people spoke to them in English and they could almost understand, yet not quite.

"I'll look up a word and you'll have to say the word," Laurita said excitedly.

"I can spell *lamp*," Kirby announced.

"Yeah, I bet." Laurita told her brothers that they would have their turns, but first she wanted Mom to give it a crack.

"Mom, say *Damascus*," began Laurita. "Just listen to the word." She repeated it slowly.

Her mother wiped her mouth with her napkin, giggled, and uttered, "Da-mas-kaz." Her mouth, usually pliable, appeared stiff.

No one laughed. They were proud of their mother trying hard words: *gearbox, telescope, persist.*

"Dad, try *fox terrier*." Laurita turned to him.

He gave it a try, his mind shifting easily as Laurita called out *semiannual, unhealthy, sparks,* and *holy-moly.*

The children were impressed, and clapped when their father not only pronounced *initiative,* but also spelled it and used it in a sentence. "I have the initiative to work and get rich in America."

The mood the next evening was different. After dinner was done, dishes done, homework almdone, and her brothers were in the bathtub, Laurita approached her father in his recliner. His eyes were half closed, like an alligator's. But she knew he was all ears and most certainly heard her footsteps. He could hear sounds from far away and could even guess whose car was starting a block away. "Oh, Señor Montez must be going to the store to get a jug of milk," he would predict.

Before she sat down next to him, he was asking, "*¿Qué quieres, mi cielo?*"

"*Papi, tengo mis papeles? Soy 'illegal?'*" Laurita asked

directly. "Do I have my papers? Am I illegal?" Her heart pounded for an answer.

"*Cómo?*" he responded, his alligator eyes now wide open. "What?"

"My papers," she repeated. "Miguel and Kirby showed me their birth certificates, but I couldn't find mine." She pointed to the desk that was like an altar, for it held a large bronze-plated candelabra and pictures from family members as far away as Jerusalem, where an aunt on her mother's side served as a nun. The desk was off limits to the kids, and was off limits to Dad as well, unless he had to fetch the digital camera hidden in the bottom drawer. It was Mom who handled all the papers, the bills, the report cards that needed to be signed, the vaccination papers, the junk mail that she read to practice her English.

With a large hand he pulled at his mouth and studied his daughter. He sat up in his recliner, buttoned the top button of his shirt, and ran a hand through his hair. He looked like a man ready to talk business.

"*Claro qué sí,*" he answered.

"But I wasn't born here, was I?" she asked.

"*No, mi'ja, naciste en Mexico,*" he answered and patted his lap, a signal for her to hop up and cuddle her old bear of a father. "You were born in Mexico. In a little house on a *ranchito*."

"What if *la migra* gets me?"

"No one's going to get you." He chuckled. "You got to remember. You're a citizen of the world." He explained that boundaries were just lines on a map and what was really important was being nice, being productive, staying in school, and honoring the country where you live.

After that, Laurita understood that she was both *Mexicana* and a citizen of the world. She had rights no matter where she lived, just as music had rights to move from country to country. Or like the folk dances they did in summer school. Or like the food they ate: one day Mexican, the next day Chinese. Why not?

Laurita wondered about birds. *Are they illegal?* she mused. They spent winters in Costa Rica but flew north to Wisconsin for summers, where they mingled with local birds. Or humpback whales: One week they were near Baja and the next month, if they swam fast enough, were in Alaska.

She was a citizen of the world. That's who she was.

One day Laurita's mother had to go to Kmart to get a few things. Laurita rode with her to the store, her mother grimacing at a rock song on the radio. It was turned low, but her mother's face was pleated with disgust.

"*¡Que horible!*" she complained.

"It's not horrible, Mom!" Laurita turned it down, but after two blocks her mother sighed and turned the volume up. She wet her lips, as if she were tasting the music, and finally concluded, "*No es Luis Miguel, pero es* okay."

At the store Laurita stayed in the car to finish reading a novel. Her mother warned her to stay put.

Laurita would have obeyed her mother, but she was curious about a commotion down the street. Loud noise made her think, *Oh, a carnival.* Then she heard barking and thought it had to be the Humane Society, which sometimes came to shopping centers to give away dogs and cats, all adorable and huggable as stuffed animals.

But it was a protest, a word she had used on Kirby when he wrote a naughty word in dirt. Hands propped on her hips, she'd admonished him. "Kirby, I protest your use of that word. You're lucky I don't tell Mom."

Laurita got out of the car and stood with one hand touching the back fender, as a gesture of safety. She understood right away: There were two groups, one waving American flags and shouting, "You Mexicans go home! You're taking our jobs! You're illegal! Go home!"

The other group, mostly young men and women, maybe some college students, was shouting, "If it wasn't for us, nothing would get done! We're the ones working! We do the hardest work!"

The two groups yelled at each other, and passersby in cars honked. The police, in glaring sunglasses, waited across the street.

Laurita, following her heart, went closer and became angry when one of the men began saying rude things about Mexico.

"You do the work!" she found herself hollering, her hands on her hips the way she did when she was mad at her brothers. "You do it!"

"That's right! I'll do the work!" the man roared. "You just go back home!"

"You're going to pick the lettuce?" Laurita inquired. "I would like to see you do that! Or, or, or—"

"You shut up, little girl!" a woman interrupted, stepping toward Laurita so that she was engulfed in the woman's shadow. The woman was wearing sunglasses and her face was smeared with white sunblock, like war paint. She had a berry-sized ruby ring on her finger. Laurita had to wonder whether the red stone contained the blood of people she had punched.

"Shut up?" Laurita asked as her hands came off her hips and wrapped around her chest. "Me shut up? That is rude, lady. Anyway, I have a right to say what I want." She stood her ground, her thin shadow falling across the sidewalk.

"You're illegal," a man in a straw hat adorned with small American flags yelled. His large belly jumped when he jumped, and his face reddened.

"Yeah, maybe," she retorted. "But I don't want to be. I'm only eleven years old!" She fumed and added, "You don't know anything!"

Laurita wheeled around, dashed to the car, and looked back at the commotion. From that distance, she remembered a word she read in a book: *tolerance*. Like getting along, like accepting, like you're white and I'm brown and both are okay. Why couldn't people be like birds or whales living without boundaries? Or seeds that fly in the wind?

Her mom, arriving with a shopping bag, scanned the crowd of protesters. The parking lot, she had said repeatedly, was more dangerous than a freeway. She muttered something in Spanish so fast Laurita believed it was a prayer.

———

After summer school ended, Laurita's father took the family on a vacation to Yosemite, an eighty-mile drive up small brownish hills that slowly became green with redwoods. Between the redwoods a river snaked through the mountains, sparkling at every turn. Hawks hung in the air, and a single cloud rode eastward on the Pacific wind. The drive was beautiful, but now and then Laurita grimaced when she saw litter on the side of the road. She brooded. *Why do people do that? Why do they have to dump trash in nature?*

They camped for two days. Her brothers, true to form, got bee stings on their faces. Bawling, they released fat tears, and her mother packed mud on their little wounds. This was an old remedy learned in Mexico, and it was useful and cheap. She poured water from a kettle onto the ground, mixed the dirt with a stick, and plastered the mud around their mouths. They looked as if they'd been eating mud, but Laurita didn't snicker.

One evening they played charades.

"Come on, Mom. You can say it," Laurita begged. She had learned the game at school, and the boys, both actors who could feign death while playing war in the yard, jumped up and down, crying, "Yeah, Mom. Come on!"

"Cha-raids," her mother tried. She had been rubbing lotion on her face to repel the mosquitoes that hovered at night.

She discovered she liked the game.

"*Quién soy yo?*" she asked during the fourth round. "Who am I?" She held a pretend object in her hand and moved it toward her mouth. Her mouth became large, then small, then a bud of lines, then large again. Her eyes shone from the fire, little red flames in each pupil. She bowed and threw a kiss, and she danced, kicking up a small puff of dust at her feet.

The boys guessed the churro guy who worked their street. Their father guessed the six o'clock news anchor on Univision. Laurita shrugged. She could come up with only someone eating a hot dog at a baseball game.

"*Ay, dios mio,*" her mother uttered. "It's so easy. I'm *American Idol.*"

The next day they started home.

"*Tu sabes,* I miss Mexican food," her father remarked as they drove down a long winding road, bugs splattering against the windshield, wind whistling through the window, something going *clunk* in the truck. While camping, they'd eaten hamburgers and grilled chicken, pork and beans, Vienna sausages, six flavors of potato chips, plus a puny fish that Miguel Dos had caught.

"*Tres días de* pork and beans! *Vamos a comer comida Mexicana en un restaurante.* We'll stop somewhere."

The kids were astonished when they stopped at a Chevys restaurant. The family seldom ate out, unless buying churros from the churro man and eating them on the curb counted.

"*Camarones para mi,*" their father crowed after he examined the menu as large as a newspaper. "It's expensive, but we're on vacation."

When the waitress came, her father looked up at her smiling face and studied her name tag.

"Madison, I would like to order," he started in stiff but correct English. "Let's start with the kids."

After the waitress left Laurita said proudly, "Dad, your English is great!" She was also proud that he hadn't remarked that the server was white, not Mexican. He didn't show prejudice.

"I'm learning." He took a sip of water. "I learn a little here and there, and everywhere." He chuckled. "Yes, everywhere. I even learn English from you three *chamacos.*"

"No, Dad. You talk like you're the president of the United States."

Her father nodded. "A piece of cake!"

Laurita's mother looked confused. Was he ordering

a piece of cake? Is that what he wanted? But her daughter explained that "a piece of cake" meant something easy.

"I'll be right back," Laurita told everyone, slinging her pink plastic purse over her shoulder. On the ride down the winding mountains toward home, Miguel Dos had somehow gotten gum in his hair. As big sister, Laurita had taken it upon herself to comb it out. Now her hands needed washing.

As she strode past the tables, she noticed a man and woman who seemed familiar. She had seen them somewhere. In the restroom, as the water bubbled over her hands, Laurita remembered where and when. They were the flag-wavers at the anti-immigration protest on the busy street in front of Kmart. The woman was the one who had shouted at her to shut up.

They don't like Mexicans, Laurita told herself, *but they want to enjoy the food. They want the people to grow the food and then prepare the food. They want them to wash the dishes and sweep the floors.*

Laurita returned to her table, cutting a quick glance at the couple. Their plates were smeared, and the woman was working food from a tooth with her finger. And there it was, on her hand: the berry-sized ruby ring.

There's blood inside it, Laurita told herself. *That*

woman should know better. She should know about nature, where birds fly, where whales swim, and how seeds float on currents to new lands. She should know that people just want to live.

But Laurita knew she was a citizen of the world, a girl who was born in Mexico, a girl who liked Chinese food, a girl who could yodel, a girl who could even dance an Irish jig.

Still, she fumed, a dark cloud of anger inside, but since they were on vacation—at least for another hour—she put on a happy face. This was another kind of charades, played in secret. The food had yet to arrive, hot and steamy. She had no intention of ruining her family's appetite for the Mexican food they knew so well.

Wise Uncle Joe

BEN FRANKLIN HAD smartly counseled other cheap-skates of his generation, "A penny saved is a penny earned." I, in turn, chanted this piece of wisdom as I went to work for Uncle Joe, a nice cheapskate. I leaped up his front steps, peered through the window of his lit-tle house, and caught him asleep with his hands across the valley of his stomach. He was bundled in two sweaters, for the thought of wasted body heat made him shiver.

I tapped on the window and called, "Uncle Joe, it's me!" Uncle Joe sat straight up like a revived corpse in a coffin, spookylike, and all bones. He smacked his lips as though he'd just realized that he was asleep, not dead. His seventy-plus ticker was still pushing blood through its chambers. Narrowing an eye at me, Uncle Joe bellowed, "You were supposed to be here this morning!"

I had intended an early-morning visit, but two friends and I had a dirt clod war in a vacant lot that concluded with me taking one to the forehead. Through the window I shouted this explanation, gently tapping the knuckle-hard lump on my skull.

"I can't hear a word you're saying!" Uncle Joe screamed. He advanced toward the door, in a bad mood. He let me in real quick to keep the furnace heat inside. We had to go through the house to the backyard—he had no gate on the side because the lumber and latches would have cost money. But first in the kitchen, he swallowed three prunes like goldfish and said, "You can have *one* if you want." He thrust a nasty-looking jar at me.

I said, "Nah, Uncle Joe, I had my Cap'n Crunch this morning. I'm here to work."

In the yard he pointed out my chore: leaves carpeting one end of the yard to the other.

"Right-o," I sang.

Instead of returning inside Uncle Joe watched my handiwork and occasionally corrected my rake action.

"When you rake, keep your elbows in," he advised.

"Why?" I questioned.

"Saves energy, and energy costs money."

Uncle Joe kept watching and swung his body into an old wicker chair. He asked if he had ever told me the story about how the tips of his boots got run over by a supply truck in the Korean War.

I told him, "Yeah, lots of times, and the one about making a broom out of twigs in 1957."

He stood up and roared, "I don't know how your teeth stay in your face, always talking that way. Don't you know how to respect your elders?"

Every thirteen-year-old boy has numerous people inside his body. Inside me lurks a smart aleck, who, I suspect, might be the real me—time will tell. I corrected my manners, and said, "Gosh, Uncle, I don't know what's wrong with my mouth," and worked the rake with my elbows in.

He burped loudly and said, "Pickles and prunes don't go together."

Disgusted, I got to work stirring up the leaves to find some air sweeter than what he had just released.

"What grade are you in?" Uncle Joe asked after he released a more polite burp.

"Seventh," I answered.

"That's a good grade," he proclaimed. "I was there two years. Had problems with math." He then clipped up the porch steps and quickly opened and closed the door—the heat loss, you know.

While he was away doing whatever old men do, I raked the yard clean and pulled up a few weeds as a punishment for smarting off. Uncle Joe returned and paced the yard, his head bowed as he inspected my work. He had slipped into yet another sweater, each button a different color and design, a sign that he had salvaged the sweater from somewhere. "Pretty fall days don't cost nothing," he quipped and smiled at the sky. I twirled the rake and muttered, "That's why you never had a girlfriend. They cost money." Then I wanted to smack my mouth for such a comment. What was wrong with me?

Uncle Joe made his busy eyebrows rise and fall. He wagged a finger at me and said, "I didn't hear what you said, but I know it was something smart-alecky. Are you makin' fun of me?" He narrowed a miserly eye, then pointed. "You missed a leaf over there."

"Nah, Uncle Joe. I respect you," I answered and retrieved the renegade leaf. And I did respect Uncle Joe, thin as a rake because he survived on nearly nothing. He lived on prunes, oatmeal, saltines, and stuff he grew in his garden. His shoes were laced with string, his eye glasses were taped at the bridge, and his chino pants were so old they were back in style. He saved rubber bands on doorknobs and was not above hunting for cans in the alley. For fun, he collected bottle caps and glued them to cardboard and played solitaire by the light of a 40-watt bulb in the kitchen.

I'm going to be nicer, I told my shameless self, *beginning now!*

When Uncle began talking about germinating tomato seeds in the first week of May, I made a thousand different faces to illustrate my interest. He gave me three quarters for my work, and I said, "Gee, Uncle Joe, I might go buy me some tomato seeds."

"What?" he asked.

I answered, "Nothing, Uncle." With one hand on the rail, Uncle Joe climbed up the porch steps and from that rickety perch gave me a wise appraisal. He asked, "Boy, how far do you think you'll go with the money I've given you over the years?" I looked around the yard, a smirk playing on my face, and I answered, "Maybe to that rosebush there or far as the orange tree."

Uncle Joe roared about how in the world I was going to make it in the world with a mouth like mine! I told him, "With dentures." With that, he came down the porch steps, twisted open my palm, and rolled those quarters back into the leathery pouch of his tightfisted hand.

I was back three days later. A few leaves had fallen from the sycamore, but Uncle Joe had a different task for me. He had gathered tin coffee can lids and ordered me to the roof. "Boy, get up there, and wherever you see weak shingles, nail down these lids. I hear it's going to rain lots."

"Who told you?" I stood at the bottom of the ladder.

"My bones. Especially my shoulder blades."

I climbed to the roof with a hammer so ancient I was sure that Thor, the Viking god of thunder, had used it to strike lightning in the fjords of Norway. The nails had been straightened out, and the wooden ladder was reinforced with rags tied around every other rung.

I did my job, climbed down, and was dusting off my palms when Uncle Joe said, "Boy, I told you about the tips of my toes getting run over by a supply truck. Did I ever show you the ribbon I earned for that tragedy?"

"Lots of times," I almost answered. But as I recalled the three quarters he had ripped from my palm, I changed my tune to, "Oh, no, Uncle Joe. Let's see."

Uncle Joe disappeared into the house and returned with a ribbon—orange and black and frayed. As I turned it over, I held it up to the light. I pressed it to my chest and said, "Gee, Uncle, it must be an honor to own it." I tried my best to pleat my face with wonder and even considered patting the frayed ribbon with a dab of spit to make it shine. Uncle would admire my thrifty action: Spit costs nothing.

"Guess what foot got run over?"

I pondered his black shoes, cracked and creased from his long strides and secured with his homemade shoelaces. They were long as the snout of an alligator.

"Your left one?" I guessed.

"Wrong!" he hollered. "It's the right one."

Soon I discovered that Uncle had a larger plan than having coffee can lids nailed on his roof or imparting another version of his history in the Korean War.

"Secretly, I'm a millionaire," he announced.

"Where do you keep your millions—in jars?"

Uncle Joe narrowed both eyes at me. "No, boy, I don't keep 'em there." He tapped his forehead and then the side of his head. "I keep 'em here. There's a million memories worth more than a million dollars."

I folded my arms across my chest and listened.

"Also, even at my age, it's not too old to become a *real* millionaire." Uncle Joe paused, expecting me to ask, "How, Uncle?"

I did.

"By invention, my young flame. And by those things over there." He pointed to what at first I thought were sticks and leaves he planned to burn in his fireplace. But I was wrong. He told me they were Christmas wreaths knitted together by his own crafty hands. He chuckled.

"What?" I asked.

He leaned his camel head near my smaller camel head. "I'm in the spirit of making money this season. How 'bout you?"

I began to wonder if Uncle Joe had been drinking a concoction stronger than the tea he kept in his jam jars.

He maintained that if people really believed in the holiday spirit, they would fork over six dollars for a homemade wreath adorned with red ribbon. Christmas, he said, was the biggest holiday, and the second biggest spending period was the week before Valentine's Day. He would brief me on that moneymaking scheme when February got closer. For now, he was fired up about Christmas wreaths.

"But if you sell all those wreaths, you couldn't become a millionaire. There's, what, a dozen of them there?"

"Got a lot more in the garage," he reported in a low voice. The fleshy territory around his mouth sagged. I had seemed to put a damper on his mood. Poor old Uncle Joe! He was seventy-something, and I, his only nephew, wasn't touting his ingenuity.

"Gosh, Uncle Joe, you might have something." I gazed at the wreaths, misshapen and plain ugly, with poorly knotted bows. But I wasn't about to mention their lack of artistry.

"Nah, I might make a few bucks."

"No, I've seen people go into the dollar store at Christmastime and come out with their arms full of these grassy things."

"Wreaths, boy. Let's improve your vocabulary." Uncle Joe stood up and stretched so his suspenders yawned on his chest. "Does it seem like it's going to rain?"

I sized up the day: cold grayness, but no hint of rain. "Nah," I answered.

"If that's the case, my young weather forecaster, how 'bout you and me see if we can sell these wreaths."

I pointed out that it was only the first week in November and that the Christmas spirit hadn't yet hit people. Jack-o'-lanterns were still sitting on porches and I hadn't seen any store windows painted with reindeer pulling Santa.

"We'll beat 'em to the punch, then," Uncle Joe said, and swung at the air.

Thirty minutes later I was hauling a small red wagon through the better part of our town. Uncle Joe had given me instructions to go up the steps, knock on the door, and hold up a wreath while I announced brightly, "Get your Christmas wreaths early!" He had also suggested that I add "ho-ho-ho" to my delivery, but I vetoed that.

At the first house, the greeter was a little girl in pajamas. She had a thumb in her mouth and a blanket over her shoulder.

"Is your mom home?" I asked.

She shook her head no.

"Your dad?"

She shook her head again.

The grandmother was home but it was no sale. The door slowly closed in my face, dangerously close to pinching my shoes. If that had happened, Uncle Joe and I would have something in common: ruined toes.

I trudged down the steps, a few needles from the wreath raining on the ground. I ventured to the next house, and the next, and next. Instead of sales or holiday spirit, I produced something close to anger on the faces of these homeowners. I did get an offer to trim a hedge and climb a roof to clean out the gutters. And I sampled a cookie baked by a really nice old lady.

I was no salesman, and my product confused a few customers. One child turned and screamed, "Mom, this boy is selling weeds. Do we need any?"

Two hours later, I had not sold a single wreath. But when I met Uncle Joe at our designated place—the mailbox on Angus Street—he was all smiles. He tossed a few raisins into his mouth and announced, "I sold five, buddy boy."

"How!" I screamed. "People said I was selling nothing but weeds."

He chuckled and gummed his raisins. There was a mischievous light in his eyes.

"What?" I asked.

"I know I shouldn't have, but I began my pitch by asking 'em to look down at my shoes." He swallowed his raisins and reported how he revealed to his customers his Korean-vet status and how his toes had been run over by a supply truck.

"Uncle! How could you!" I screamed. The scam artist! This approach struck me as dishonorable, although why, I wasn't sure. His story was partly true—this much I know because I had seen his toes, which were long and flat from the weight of a four-ton truck. Still, it didn't seem right, taking advantage of people's sympathy for veterans when there were veterans in *real* need.

"How much you sell again?" he inquired with a chuckle. Before I could answer truthfully, he made an okay sign with his fingers, which for him meant zero.

"How did you know?" I barked.

Uncle Joe cleared his throat and said, "Boy, you need an angle."

We parted. I skipped a few houses where dogs with crazy eyes dwelled behind chain-link fences. But at one pretty house, I climbed the stairs, ran my fingers through my unruly hair, and announced to the person who opened the door, "Ma'am, we're having a school fund drive for the poor." The woman closed the door none too softly.

At the next house, I said, "Ma'am, we're keeping youth off drugs." This door closed quicker, the breeze adjusting the curls on my head. Still not ready to admit defeat, I braved the next house. "Ma'am, we're here early because cats need loving homes." The woman narrowed her eyes at me, then scanned the wreath in my hand and asked, "Are you selling bushes?" Before

I could answer, "No, ma'am, we're selling preseason Christmas wreaths," she closed the door on me.

I was out of luck, and my sample wreath was now nearly as bald as Uncle Joe.

I dragged my red wagon down the uneven sidewalk, each bump shaking more needles from the wreaths. I had no energy to combat the sneering laughter of a kid asking, "Hey, ugly, how come you're hauling bushes around?" No, I kept my eyes cast on the sidewalk, which soon revealed a large shadow. When I looked up, it was a smiling Uncle Joe.

"Sold 'em all!" He did a jig on his gimpy legs.

"Great," I managed to say.

Uncle Joe looked down at my wreaths. He asked, "Hey, what did you do? Strangle the wreaths?" He picked one up as if it were a baby and put it back down gently. He picked up another and examined this one, too, mumbling complaints about the bald wreaths. Finally he settled on the best of my bunch and beckoned me to follow him.

"I told this lady that I would put one on the front of her car."

"What do you mean?" I asked.

"You'll see," he said vaguely. He walked two blocks

before we stopped our parade in front of a very nice house. On the front door, I noticed, hung one of his wreaths.

"Looks real smart," Uncle Joe bragged.

I had to admit that the wreath on the door was a nice touch, even though Uncle Joe wasn't worth a million dollars. Still, he had bills and coins in his pocket and they weren't about to come out soon! The guy was too stingy.

"You wait here," he ordered. He climbed the steps and visited with the homeowner, a mother with two children wrapped around her ankles like snakes. He descended with a whistle on his lips.

"She says it's okay," he announced.

"What's okay?"

Uncle Joe didn't elaborate. He just drew a length of wire from his pocket and tied the wreath to the grille of the Volvo station wagon in the driveway. He explained this was the style—not only did people put wreaths on their doors, but also displayed their Christmas spirit by attaching them to their cars.

"It's neat, huh?" Uncle Joe added that the woman had bought two wreaths because of his war injury.

"What did you tell her?"

"Nothing, really." Boyishly, he kicked at the ground,

a sign of embarrassment, and jingled the coins in his deep pockets.

"You told her a lie, huh?"

Uncle Joe dramatically snorted. "Boy, you got to learn how to talk to your elders." He then confessed that, indeed, he had extended the boundaries of truth by informing his customer that he'd had the tips of *both* shoes run over.

"You didn't," I admonished.

"I did, and I feel bad." He pouted.

"How could you?" I scolded.

He shrugged and muttered that he'd been wrong to fib, but he needed the money because his injury cost him more than an ugly foot. When he bought shoes (every six years), he had to buy one in size nine and the other in size ten. His flattened toes needed more room to breathe, he explained.

We walked up the street, now growing dim, but Uncle was still in the mood to make money. He scooted the wreaths from the wagon into the gutter. In their place he started tossing in aluminum cans from the neighborhood trash cans, after stomping them flat in a crazy dance.

"Uncle, I got to go," I announced after ten minutes of this kind of work.

"Go?" he barked. "There's money to make."

"You make it," I said.

He gave me one of his narrow-eyed stares until I groaned and agreed to help.

We canvassed the gutters and trash cans until the wagon chimed like music as we hauled our loot down the street. Uncle Joe said that life was hard, but if you didn't have to pay for it, it was good.

"What does that mean?" I asked.

"Think about it, boy," Uncle Joe advised. "I'm not sure myself, but I know there's truth in my words."

Like Ben Franklin, he knew about pennies, as each can we scavenged was worth a few of them. And no can was going to be passed up.

"Get that one in the road," he commanded. He pointed to an aluminum can in the street and I hurried to retrieve it. While I was bending over, a three-eyed car moved toward me. The middle headlight appeared to be blazing. I righted myself and muttered, "What the heck!"

It was only after the vehicle surged past me that I understood that the headlight *was* blazing.

"Did you see that?" I called to Uncle Joe, who appeared confounded by the car that had just passed. He raked a hand over his sharp chin. He munched on his lower lip as if in deep thought. Uncle's mind, I could see even in that early dusk, was at work. He spit sharply at the ground and remarked, "Yeah, boy, I did."

We watched the car stop at the corner, then speed down the street, throwing off a light like dawn peering over a mountain.

"I think it was the Volvo with—" I started.

"You don't have to tell me." Uncle Joe came alive, grabbed the handle of the wagon loaded with aluminum cans, and commanded, *"Vámanos!"*

The third eye of the Volvo was the wreath Uncle Joe had attached to the grille. Made of combustible twigs, it had caught fire. While it was an honest mistake by my well-meaning uncle, we felt like fugitives and galloped away.

"Are we in trouble?" I asked.

"Depends," he answered, and pocketed his dentures so he wouldn't lose them if we actually had to sprint.

Several times, at the sighting of cop cars, we were forced to hide behind bushes until we were soiled and drenched in sweat from throwing ourselves onto the ground. But we got home without incident.

We had to wait a whole worrisome day before we found ourselves in the news. Uncle Joe and I went down to the library to read a small article in the newspaper—

buying a paper would be a reckless expenditure of money!

I broke the silence as we walked down the steps of the library. "Uncle, they could have gotten hurt." We had read in the article that an unknown scam artist was working the neighborhood, selling dry flammable wreaths. I could tell that Uncle Joe resented the implication: scam artist! Uncle was stingy and occasionally a weaver of stories that were not entirely true. But at heart he was honest.

Later, when we huddled at his small kitchen table, he poured the weakest of weak teas into a jam jar and pushed it with a knuckle in my direction. He had used an old tea bag, and I swore that the staple that held it together was rusty. But I kept my lip buttoned. Neither of us was in the mood to argue over something as meaningless as a tea bag.

"Drink up," he ordered.

Darkness at last climbed the kitchen walls. The wind rattled the windows, and the neighbor's cat walked the fence like a sentry.

Uncle Joe, head bowed, spoke into his weak tea. "I guess you live and learn." He tapped a finger against the kitchen table, and I could see that he was reflecting on the near tragedy of a woman driving her Volvo unaware that her grille had become a grill on which you could barbecue. He sighed deeply, raked his whiskery chin with his hand, and shook his large camel head.

We sat in silence, we sat in shame, and finally we sat in darkness. Uncle Joe rose and turned on the overhead light, then spoke up.

"Did I ever tell you 'bout a comrade of mine who parachuted into the arms of a beautiful Irish lassie? World War Two, that was." He took a sip of tea and recounted the story of Fred Flitter, a foot soldier who was assigned to an airborne unit because he was chubby and everyone figured that if he hit the ground hard he could roll like a meatball and come up shooting. On the first day of a practice run, he parachuted right into the arms of a very strong local beauty.

I hadn't heard that one. I listened, now and then sipping my tea and trying to dismiss the fear that I might get lockjaw from the rusty staple in the tea bag.

"It was fun time for ol' Fred." He chortled. Uncle Joe told me that this guy Fred Flitter learned to shear sheep from this Irish lassie. Uncle pulled his chair away from the table and began to shave an invisible sheep, his hand making a swooping motion, all the while imitating the buzzing sound of a razor. With each uplifting stroke he increased the volume.

"This was 1944," Uncle Joe recalled. "Hitler was on the run, and the war was almost over. Fred parachuted again weeks later and twisted an ankle. The old fellow earned the same injury ribbon as me." His mood had improved mightily. He drank his tea, smacked his lips, and bellowed, "Let me show you again! No telling when it'll come in handy." He bent over and began to run an invisible razor over an invisible sheep. He made the buzzing sound and even shook out the invisible sheep wool. Soon I was called to imitate sheepshearing; after all, there was no telling when it would come in handy.

"More wrist action, boy," Uncle Joe scolded. "Put something behind it!" He shuffled to the refrigerator and brought out a cloudy jar of prunes. He downed two, permitted himself a soft and painless fart, and returned to the kitchen table. He began a yarn about another Fred, someone named Fred Salinas, a man with arms like anvils and the tiny waist of an ant. But I cleverly tuned Uncle Joe out by making my lips buzz like a giant razor while I concentrated on my sheepshearing.

"Boy, are you listening?" Uncle Joe scolded.

"Yes, sir!" I answered, startled from my musings.

"I'm telling you 'bout Fred Salinas. Man who saved our nation in spring of 1944." Uncle Joe poked my shoulder with a finger. "How come you're so soft?"

"Because I'm tenderhearted," I answered.

"Tenderhearted!" he roared. "That will set you back, boy! Don't you know this is a dog-eat-dog world—and quit with that buzzing noise! What's wrong with you?"

So, late on an autumn day, I learned to shear an invisible sheep, absorbed monotonous stories about Fred Flitter and Fred Salinas, and as Uncle's last order for the day, raked leaves in the near dark. For my labor in the backyard, Uncle said if I found a penny, nickel, dime, or quarter in the grass, we could split it. How? I don't know. But I'm sure that wise Uncle Joe would have found a way.

Seeing the Future

AT THIRTEEN, Letty Rodriguez had fallen for Miguel Padilla. He was nice. That's what she liked about him, and that he was funny. He was not super handsome, but girls thought he was a catch. Letty's catch. While she was a top student in her seventh-grade classes, he was barely making it through eighth grade. His grades, already inflated because he was a charmer with the teachers, were mostly Ds and Cs. He blamed the situation on his home life: His father was gone, his mother worked a lot at the packing shed, and his two brothers and sister were noisy as pirates. He couldn't study with the television blaring and his mother on his case about one thing or another. Letty would suggest tenderly, "Miguel, you could study at the library."

"The *liberry* is for little kids," he would argue, and go off with friends to play soccer.

Letty thought Miguel was a keeper, even if she used her allowance to make him happy: Big Gulp sodas, candies and potato chips, tickets to movies that she didn't really want to see, like the one about snakes on a plane. But he was nice and funny, and she liked his hair. And there was a sensitive side to him.

"Yeah, I like flowers," he had once remarked. He sucked his Big Gulp through a straw and related how he and his friend Richard used to pick their neighbor's flowers and give them to their mothers. He sucked again on the Big Gulp, rattled the ice, and said, "You want some?"

Letty's heart swelled the afternoon he surprised her with flowers. True, they were artificial ones from a yard sale, but it was the thought that counted.

Letty even wrote Miguel a poem in gold ink.

"That's sweeeet," he crowed. With roving eyes he studied the poem. Letty assumed he was looking for its meaning until he asked, "Hey, is that real gold?"

She took care of him by patting medicine on his forehead after he fell off his skateboard. "Poor baby," she cooed.

"I got me a scar," he responded proudly. "Puts a little edge on me. People be asking, 'Who did that to you?' and I'm going to say, 'Some dude now in the grave.'"

When they couldn't go to the theater because her allowance was used up, they watched movies at Letty's house. With his shoes off and his hand on his belly, Miguel was a king in the recliner. He would dip his hand into a bowl of buttered popcorn. The remote would be greasy when he left, and Letty's father would grumble, "That kid."

But Letty began to notice a change in Miguel. When he saw her between classes, he wouldn't rush to her anymore. Instead, he would hitch up his pants and stroll over with Richard or some other homie at his side.

Invariably he would ask, "You got any money, Letty?"

One day he approached her with smooches.

"Dawg, not so fast," she cooed. Her heart was beating, but her mind was calculating the reason for his sudden affection.

"I got to ask for a favor," Miguel said with his arms around her shoulders.

Her heart slowed. He's going to ask for money, she predicted. She had told him that her godmother had given her two hundred dollars for her birthday. His noodle of a brain had no memory for schoolwork, but when it came to money, he remembered.

"What is it?" she asked cautiously. Her hands were on his biceps, which she noticed were not taut with muscle but flabby. The result of devouring candies and sodas? She felt a little guilty about embracing him while thinking, *Just push the dude away and run!*

"I was gonna get my class ring," he began, then stopped to holler to a friend that he would see him at four at the courts. "My mom got sick," he continued with a weak smile, "and she was supposed to buy it for me." He stopped and waited, his eyes shifting away from her when someone called, "Hey, Miguel, you ugly fool." It was a homie friend with a sucker in the corner of his mouth.

"But Miguel," Letty whimpered in a little-girl voice. She explained that the ring cost over a hundred dollars, maybe two hundred, and she was saving her money for something special.

"Fool, where we be meeting?" the homie hollered.

Letty winced. She had started not to like his friends, and how he was always trying to cuddle up to her when he needed something. Even if he wanted a bag of potato chips, he would hold her hand and try to kiss her. He would leave grease on her throat, which made her queasy. "Why do you let him call you that?"

"Homegirl, they ain't nowhere," Miguel replied as he took her hand and applied a greasy kiss.

He moved his face toward her throat, but she pushed him away. She barked, "I'm not your homegirl. I'm your girlfriend."

"That's what I'm saying," he said, his shoulders lifting and his arms spreading out. "Just a loan, Letty. We're tight."

Letty began to think she could do better than a boyfriend like Miguel. But could she? She was slightly overweight, with a pinch of baby fat around her middle. No matter how she cut back on junk food, it stayed. And while people said she was cute, no one went as far as saying that she was beautiful. She was smart. This much she knew. She was the one with a row of As on her report card to back up the rumors about her intelligence.

Are we tight? she wondered. Should she lend him the money, or save it for an academic summer camp? A school counselor had suggested she apply for a summer program at San Jose State. There, she could take a class in architecture, an interest of hers ever since she'd watched a PBS special on the Roman Empire. She had watched part of it with Miguel, who only said, "I wonder if those Roman dudes had, like, lowrider chariots, all tricked out."

But Letty was still convinced that he was nice and funny. Plus, there was his hair, and he was popular. But her conscience nagged her. *He's a user, girl,* part of her mind told her. *He's trying to use you and then drop you.*

She had left him that afternoon promising to think about the loan.

"What's there to think about?" he asked later as he walked at her side, his hand pulling up the back of his pants every fifth step. "We're tight." He told her he would get the ring, but she could wear it on a chain around her neck.

At the time, Letty didn't think of the chain as being similar to the ones binding the hands and ankles of prisoners in old movies. She didn't consider the class ring a rock that would weigh her down. No, she imagined the ring around her neck as evidence of attachment, a sign to others that she had a guy. Still, she had to ponder her relationship with Miguel. Hadn't she already lent him twenty dollars? And why had she? To feed his fool friends?

"I'll think about it," she told him.

Letty had to hurry home because her mother wanted her to come along on a visit to her grandmother, who had had surgery for the removal of a tumor. All had gone well, but a visit would perk Grandmother up.

"How are you, Grandma?" Letty asked as she bent over the woman for a gentle hug. Letty wasn't sure if a hardy squeeze might hurt her.

"Okay, *mi'ja*," her grandmother answered softly. On the table beside her was a Big Gulp, which reminded Letty of Miguel. The rings on her grandmother's fingers also reinforced her memory of Miguel. "Can you get me some ice?" her grandmother asked. Her head swiveled toward the Big Gulp.

In the kitchen Letty stalled at the refrigerator when her cell jangled. She examined Miguel's number and couldn't help but think, *It looks like a prison number.* She chuckled as she pocketed her cell and admonished herself for such an unkind thought.

When she returned, her grandmother and mother were revisiting a family hurt that went back years. They did this often, hissing like snakes, pulling in their fangs only when others were around. The two became quiet as Letty entered the bedroom.

"Oh, thank you," Grandmother said as she took the Big Gulp cup. "How's school?"

"Good. I'm saving my money for a summer program at State." She had begun to explain her interest in architecture when her grandmother demanded, "How come your hair is so short? Do you like boys?"

Letty was perturbed that her grandmother hadn't listened. And what was this about not liking boys? She bristled when her mother said, "Boys like long hair."

But Letty checked her emotions and held in her disappointment. Was this her family?

"Elena," her grandmother began. Letty considered correcting her grandmother by saying, "No, I'm Leticia," but she figured her grandmother's memory was perforated with holes. She had six other grandchildren. She couldn't get their names right every time.

Her grandmother sipped from the Big Gulp and smacked her lips. "Could you walk the dog?"

The pug was curled up on the rug in the corner of the bedroom. Poor Sammy, a loyal dog, was mostly imprisoned indoors and just plain old. Letty was glad to leave the house. She got the leash from the kitchen and whistled. "Come on, Sammy. Let's go for a walk."

Her grandmother lived across the street from a park. Fall leaves carpeted the lawn. The trees rattled their remaining leaves, and the afternoon sun blazed weakly. The squeak of the swings reminded Letty of her childhood and how her father would push her high.

She paused when her cell rang. *It's Miguel,* she thought, and didn't bother to bring the phone out of her front pocket.

Letty parked herself on a bench and let Sammy roam the lawn, nibble at a flea in his fur, and poke his flat nose into a puddle of water. When she got up and clapped her hands, the dog didn't look up.

"Poor thing," she murmured. "He can hardly hear anymore." When she called the dog loudly, he hurried to join her at the swings. She kicked herself up to a dizzying height. But it wasn't the same as when her father had pushed her and the cold sang through her hair and froze her ears.

She jumped from the swing when Sammy began to wander toward a couple pushing a stroller. "Sammy, come back," she ordered. She slapped her thighs and whistled, but the dog advanced toward the couple.

Silly dog, she thought, and began running, something she hadn't done in a long time and that made her feel like a little kid. There was happiness inside her— she, a thirteen-year-old, chasing after a dog. Was there anything happier in life?

As she got closer, she recognized the young woman— a girl who had moved away from the neighborhood a year ago. *Oh, my gosh,* Letty thought as her trot slowed to a walk. The girl was maybe sixteen and already had a baby in a stroller. The scene struck Letty like a revelation and sent chills racing down her back. The young mother hadn't gotten rid of her own baby fat—it was around her middle and eventually, Letty suspected, would spread down her thighs and wobble up her arms. It was only a matter of time.

"Sorry." Letty flashed a quick smile as she lifted Sammy into her arms.

But neither of them responded. There were tears in the girl's eyes and something like boredom in the boy's. Neither turned to coo loving words to the baby who had begun to cry and kick its pink blanket.

Letty hurried away. She dropped on the lawn, released Sammy from her hold, and glanced at the couple, now sitting on a far bench. The baby was crying, and neither made the effort to bring the baby into their arms and comfort her with baby talk.

"I'm not going to be like them," she told herself. She was going to save her money for the architecture class at San Jose State.

A leaf floated down from a eucalyptus tree and tapped her shoulder. She crushed it in her palm, and the rush of childhood returned when she closed her eyes and breathed in its aroma. She wove a ring out of grass and slipped it onto her finger, then made a small grassy crown for Sammy. She could see for herself that she was only thirteen and had a future. No matter how often Miguel called, she wasn't answering.

The Ideal City

REBECCA MARTINEZ was gazing into her lunch bag—sandwich, carrot sticks, and three star-shaped cookies (all broken but still sweet)—when Sylvia Gonzalez set a piece of paper on her desk. At first Rebecca assumed Sylvia was showing off an old report card. Then she thought, *It looks like a claim check for the dry cleaners.* But that didn't seem right, either. What was it?

"My dad said you could fix it," Sylvia stated boldly.

Sylvia was the newly appointed president of the sixth-grade class. She had been promoted when the previous president moved away, taking with him the rumor that he had stolen the ice cream money during a fire drill.

"What do you mean, 'fix it'?" Rebecca asked.

"You know."

Rebecca shrugged. She didn't know.

Sylvia sighed in frustration, her breath blowing across Rebecca's arm.

Yuck, Rebecca thought. Her mouth curled up in disgust as she wiped her arm.

"Let me tell you, then." Sylvia explained that her father had gotten a citation for parking in a yellow zone—he was there only three minutes!—and since Rebecca's mom, the only parking enforcement in their dinky town, was the person who had issued the citation, she could get rid of it.

Rebecca gripped the throat of her paper bag, choking it as if it had done something wrong. Wouldn't her mom get in trouble? What Sylvia was seeking was against the law.

"I can't do that," Rebecca replied. "I don't know how."

"It happens all the time," Sylvia confided in a near whisper. "Your mom can fix it!"

Rebecca shrugged. At that, Sylvia grew angry but remained cautious, as her eyes shifted occasionally to their teacher, Mrs. Lynch. If Mr. Gonzalez had to pay the parking ticket, Sylvia divulged, he wouldn't have the money to get her the coat he promised.

Again Rebecca repeated her moral stance: No, she couldn't help.

"Do it," Sylvia snarled. Her eyes became stoked with anger.

Rebecca stepped back, frightened. The clock over the white board read 11:57. In three minutes she would be out the door and rushing toward the table where she always ate lunch with her best friend, Carolina.

"You can too!" Sylvia was grim. "Just ask your mother!"

Rebecca whirled around and fled, her hands touching each desk as she made her way up the row. She felt dizzy with fear.

Because Carolina had to stay in class to make up a test, Rebecca ate alone. She wondered about her poor mother. She worked in parking enforcement and drove a little vehicle—half car, half scooter—a job that provided them with a house and food. For her efforts, she was often yelled and spat at and twice pushed. *Why do they blame her?* Rebecca argued. It was just her mom's job.

As she finished her lunch, she kept her distance from the other students. From where she sat, she recognized danger: Two boys were fighting and Sylvia was right in the mix, her fists swinging.

Rebecca was then surprised by a third grader in a dirty Disneyland T-shirt. He demanded the cookie in her hand, and she handed him a piece.

He turned it over, baring his teeth like a shark, and remarked, "You got ugly cookies." He fit it into his mouth, turned, and left.

Rebecca's heart sank. If she were president of her class, she would mandate that kids with dirty hands be taught manners!

"They're not ugly," she muttered. She nibbled the other half of the broken cookie, hurt because the boy spoke the truth. Unlike fancier Oreos and Nutter Butters, the cookies her mother bought were cheaper and poorer quality. Still, they were sweet, not like Sylvia. Not like a lot of people.

On the way home Rebecca spied Sylvia standing at a corner with two large girls. They were eating potato chips and doughnuts and sharing a forty-eight-ounce soda.

"They're going to get me," she murmured, her heart fluttering like a little bird behind her blouse. She gazed up into the tree; a bird was chirping a sad sound.

Rebecca tiptoed backward, hid behind a car, and, when it was safe, leaped across the street. She took a new route home.

It was a scary odyssey. Large dogs behind chain-link fences snorted and showed their teeth, slobber hanging from the corners of their mouths. There were car parts on almost every yellowish lawn, and if not car parts, old couches, rusty swings, parts of refrigerators, dismantled bicycles, deflated blow-up swimming pools, and broken toys. There were men on porch steps, their eyes cloudy. None of them smiled at her, although one man waved a flyswatter in her direction. Rebecca didn't understand why he was doing that, and she didn't hang around to find out.

She hurried away, skipped even, hoping to look carefree. But she soon slowed to a walk and played a game: Step on a crack and break your mother's back. She treaded carefully, heel to toe, but froze when she again spied Sylvia with her friends. They were dragging sticks in the gutter, gathering leaves wet as paper towels.

Rebecca turned and ran. Two blocks later she was forced sit on the curb and rest. She recalled the singsong phrase "Sticks and stones may break my bones, but words will never hurt me." But she didn't believe it. Words do hurt, and so do songs with bad words. She knew nasty people walked the earth doing bad. There were wars, famines, and earthquakes that destroyed villages in remote fog-shrouded valleys. Rebecca felt stranded in one of those valleys, crying, "Help, help, help me!"

"You're too sensitive," her grandmother had once scolded. "That's your problem." Her grandmother made this remark after Rebecca had cried at the scene of a hippopotamus bellowing for her hippo child that had been eaten by a lion. They had been watching a show on Animal Planet about how animals, like humans, could feel grief.

What had the mother hippo done to make her grandmother resent its grief? *Poor hippo*, Rebecca thought. *Poor, poor hippo.*

At home, Rebecca reveled in an Animal Planet special about a kindly veterinarian who helped chimpanzees in the wilds of Zimbabwe. They exuded happiness. They beat their chests with pleasure, jumped up and down, and showed their large teeth. The chimpanzees shared what they had and groomed each other, pulling crawly things from their matted hair. The program soothed her, and some cold lemonade made her feel better, too.

"Animals are a lot nicer than people," she concluded.

Rebecca planned to watch the next program about a giraffe until she remembered her chore: make a green salad to go with leftover creamy chicken from dinner the night before. Afterward, she took out a large binder that held her extra-credit project about saving the world. To Rebecca it was all so obvious. If adults and kids did a few simple things, they could save the world for future generations.

On butcher paper Rebecca drew the Ideal City. She placed parks every five blocks. She colored the parks blue because she couldn't find the green crayon, but she figured that blue was the color of the sky (when not smoggy) and the sea (when not dirty with oil spills). She dotted her made-up world with trees, also blue, and made a note in the margin explaining that these were fruit trees. She predicted that people would give up candy and turn to eating fruit because such trees would be everywhere in the city. They could look up at any time, say, "Oh, an apple," and pluck it for free.

"No police or soldiers!" she demanded. She took out a pencil and scrawled this directive in the margin. The people would be polite because they would have lots to eat and places to live. But if people weren't nice, flying drones would zap them with bolts of electricity. *It's going to hurt,* she told herself, *but the drones won't kill them, just zap them to make them behave.*

"We'll need to have swimming pools," she pledged. She began to make little blue squares and then a long blue line: a river, clean, sparkly, and filled with fish. Citizens would fish when the fruit trees became bare in late fall. Rebecca felt guilty that some of the fish would have to die. But it couldn't be helped, she figured. The citizens of the Ideal City had to eat.

The phone rang. When Rebecca picked it up, the caller—Rebecca was certain it was Sylvia—hung up.

After they washed the dishes, Rebecca and her mother watched *Jeopardy,* a program they relished because they would get wild and scream out their questions, each pushing a make-believe button. It gave them joy, competing in a nice way. Rebecca made a mental note: In the Ideal City people would watch Animal Planet or *Jeopardy,* or something new, like the Star Planet channel or a game show based on Candyland.

"What is Wyoming!" they screamed at the same time.

"No, I said it first," Rebecca claimed.

The answer was a state where Yellowstone National Park is located.

The previous summer they had visited the park and had been dazzled by the depth of the night sky and its pulsating stars. They had a decal from Yellowstone on the back window of their Toyota Corolla. It was starting to peel, but the memory was still there. A bear had sauntered up to their car and laid its heavy paws on the hood, rolled its large petallike tongue over its mouth, and demanded something to eat.

When *Jeopardy* was over, Rebecca revealed her problem at school. "This girl, she's, like, mean but the president of our class. She wants me to get you to fix a ticket or her dad won't buy her a new jacket."

Her mother picked up her soda from the TV tray and drank its strawberry sweetness, but she didn't pick up the thread of the conversation. She just looked at her daughter, expecting more.

"This girl is mean, Mom. I know she beat up at least three girls this year and made a boy cry when she took his lunch."

"Narrow-minded," her mother finally added. "People think I can do that—everyone, even your aunt." Rebecca's mother recounted how Aunt Norma had called her to ask if she could fix a parking ticket for her new boyfriend. Absently she added, "Everyone wants something for free."

The two had been full of laughter, but now their mood had changed. Rebecca got up to turn on the lamp on the end table, but the light didn't brighten the tone.

"What should I do?" Rebecca asked.

"'Bout what?"

"The girl at school. She's bothering me."

"Ignore her," Rebecca's mother advised. She turned off the television and a smiling face selling toothpaste disappeared. "Did you do your homework?"

"I don't have any homework." Rebecca was going to reveal her school project—the Ideal City—when the phone rang. She gripped the arm of the couch, not unlike their cat when she tried to put it outside, then got up and answered the phone.

"Hello," Rebecca greeted. "Hello, hello?"

Silence, two clicks, a faraway sort of silence—was Sylvia trying to play with her head? Right then Rebecca considered another possibility: no telephones in the Ideal City. If a person wanted to talk to another person, he or she would have to knock on his or her door.

"As president of the class, I would like to thank you for your visit." Sylvia smiled at Dr. Sharon Dietz, who was only a little taller than the average sixth grader. Her hair was bushy red and her face looked orange against her white lab coat. The doctor had been invited to talk to the fifth and sixth graders about good eating habits. "As a token of our appreciation, we hope that you will accept our school T-shirt."

Dr. Dietz accepted the T-shirt from the beaming Sylvia and held it in front of her like a matador's cape.

She waved the T-shirt and jumped to the side as if a bull were rushing toward her.

Sylvia's so fake, Rebecca surmised. *Isn't it obvious?*

The program over, the students rose noisily from the benches, and the teachers began to escort them from the cafeteria. But Sylvia stayed behind for a photo op with the doctor and the dental hygienist, who had brought a huge set of teeth that opened and closed like a clam. The hygienist had used them to demonstrate how to floss. He had warned them about the harmfulness of sugar and the gunk that gets trapped between teeth. With a large toothbrush he had demonstrated how to brush with an up-and-down action.

Rebecca was mildly upset that this person didn't receive a T-shirt. The poor guy stood to the side, the huge set of teeth in his arms. The teeth seemed to smile at the students shuffling away, and a few of the nastier boys bared their teeth at the man.

"They're awful." Rebecca sighed. She vowed they would be the first to get zapped by the flying drones in the Ideal City.

When Rebecca filed past, she waved vigorously to the man. He didn't see her at first, but then he rigged a big smile on his face. Right then she decided that if she could really build the Ideal City, he would be mayor.

He seemed nice and was young enough to remember what it felt like in school. If he were mayor—no, she'd make him governor or even president of the Ideal City—the citizens would be assured of sparkling teeth and healthy gums.

After the assembly the sixth graders had silent reading, but the silence was broken when the speaker next to the clock crackled, buzzed, and seemed to belch. The entire class looked up.

"Sixth graders, the freezer has broken." The voice belonged to Mr. Rafferty, the vice principal.

There was a roar of excitement. It was only 10:34 in morning, and for the second time that day they got to leave the classroom. This was way better than a talk about health: The broken freezer meant they got to help eat the school's supply of ice cream before it melted.

They lined up with Sylvia first—as president, she assumed she would lead. She elbowed the boy behind her, barking, "Get off me, stupid! You're standing too close." Then, like a centipede, the students left the classroom boisterously yelling like it was Christmas.

In the cafeteria they were each presented with an ice cream—Drumsticks and Push-ups, Popsicles and Eskimo Pies—and a single napkin.

"Goof off and you're back in the classroom," warned

Mr. Rafferty, a skinny man with a twig for a neck. He didn't look like he could have enough strength to back up his words.

The students knew they had to be quiet just for the time it took to devour a frosty concoction. They formed a circle as he had instructed and ate the icy treats, the only sound the slobber of ice cream being devoured.

But Rebecca didn't indulge in the ice cream feed. She was determined to follow the wise instruction of the dental hygienist. *Excess sugar is bad for you,* she told herself.

"How come you're not eating?" Carolina asked.

"I'm not hungry," she answered.

Rebecca waited and tried to avoid staring at Sylvia gobbling nastily on a green Popsicle. She had higher concerns and tinkered in her mind with the finer details of the Ideal City. She figured that in the future people would eat less, not more, so there would be hardly any deaths. Everyone would live for something close to forever. True, they would get old and move slower, but they would go on and on.

Provided they ate less and flossed weekly.

A week passed, and Rebecca was continually bullied by Sylvia, who would cut her down with icy stares, hiss dirty words, toss balled-up napkins at her in the cafeteria, and threaten her with a good ol' school yard whipping.

One day mean Sylvia chased her around the school yard, her cheeks filled with water from the drinking fountain.

"Don't!" Rebecca pleaded. She was cornered near the baseball backstop, jumping left, then right as she attempted to avoid the inevitable. "Don't! I'll tell! I really will!" Rebecca was grossed out—they had just eaten lunch and most likely there were loose food particles in Sylvia's fat cheek. *Yuck, that water is dirty. I might even get a disease*—all this and more entered Rebecca's mind.

Sylvia let the stream fly from her mouth, and it splashed on Rebecca's leg.

"That was really mean!" Rebecca cried. She limped in a circle, and pouted because her sock was wet.

But when Rebecca reported what Sylvia had done, Mr. Rafferty had a greater concern than a girl who'd been spit on—a boy had climbed up to the roof in an effort to fetch a kickball and now couldn't get down.

On the way home Rebecca would chant in her heart, "Sticks and stones may break my bones, but words will never hurt me."

For the next few days, Rebecca avoided Sylvia. She

hung with her friend Carolina, playing two-square with a nearly deflated ball. Carolina was quicker, more competitive, and just plain better.

Rebecca realized that competition made her sullen—and sweaty! At home, she added another improvement in the margins of the map of the Ideal City: no competition. She rationalized that competitive sports made people go crazy—just look at professional football, a sport that made people dress up in weird clothes and cuss at the ref. Was that civilized?

In the Ideal City people would just play catch or they could swim. Yes, they would swim laps. She mulled over other activities.

"We can juggle," she said to herself. She wrote in the margins *juggle, hula hoop, ride ponies, run through sprinklers,* and that thing called *yoga*: noncompetitive stuff.

That night, with the television muted and her mother seated in her recliner, Rebecca practiced her presentation of the Ideal City. For ten minutes she outlined her major points and explained the rules for living in peace and love.

"What would you think if there were no litter and stuff?" Rebecca asked.

"But, honey, is there really a place like—" Rebecca's

mother started to discount this magical place, then reigned in her opinion. Every day she rode around and saw gutters filled with garbage.

Mom's a doubter, Rebecca figured, *but that's okay because the Ideal City is still only on paper.* Rebecca was convinced that once her plans became a reality everyone would start to act nicer. Everyone would change. Then her mother would see.

The next day she walked to school clutching her report and the butcher paper on which she had drawn the map.

After the first recess Rebecca began her presentation by showing the class pictures of the Hawaiian Islands.

"Would you like to live in paradise?" she asked. "Right under a coconut tree?"

A classmate raised his hand and asked, "Para—what?"

Rebecca was not disturbed by this interruption, or the fact that the boy had orange Cheeto stains at the corners of his mouth.

"Good question," she replied. She gave a summary of their terrible times: wars and famines, cars all over the place, oil from the cars in driveways, and earthquakes where people had to lie under rubble for days and days. "This can all change."

Rebecca noticed that her teacher, Mrs. Lynch, was at her desk, making small but fierce checks on their math problems. Mrs. Marshall, the teacher's aide who worked in the classroom in the afternoons, was looking through her purse. *They're not listening,* she surmised, and this hurt because Mrs. Lynch had oohed and aahed when she'd first heard about the project. But now the teacher didn't seem to care. Still, Rebecca hung a toothy smile on her face.

"See, I have drawn a map of the city." She pointed with a ruler. "I call it the Ideal City. Later it'll have another name."

She showed the map by walking from one side of the class to the other. Her confidence grew. Her classmates, even Sylvia, were examining the map.

A kid remarked, "It don't look like our city."

"That's right!" Rebecca nearly screamed in delight. "That's because it's nicer. The Ideal City will have parks everywhere and a river. Don't you wish you could fish in a river?"

Her classmates seemed unmoved by the portrait of paradise.

"If you don't like fishing, there would be other things to do." She cast light on her plans: The parks would be the greenest green, and each tree would have a bird's nest, maybe two.

Yawns from two students.

"The birds will have more freedom than ever," Rebecca exclaimed. She flung her arms into the air. "They'll pull up worms and wouldn't have to eat garbage because no one would litter anymore. Won't that be nice?"

No response.

In desperation, she called out, "And Sylvia!"

Sylvia had been chewing a fingernail, her head bowed. When she gazed up, her mouth was red, as if she had been feeding on blood. But it was only the stain of candy.

"Sylvia, there aren't going to be any parking tickets. You can tell your dad that." Rebecca crossed her heart and said, "I promise."

Sylvia's scowl produced deep rivulets of hatred around her mouth.

"Don't be mad! Didn't you hear me? *No parking tickets.*"

Sylvia puffed out her cheeks as if they held water or the biggest gob of spit in the world. Rebecca rocked back on her heels. She stepped quickly to the other side of the classroom.

There would be no cars in the Ideal City, Rebecca announced after she shuffled her notes. People would get around by walking or bicycling. True, a single ambulance for really old people would be needed, but most people would be so healthy they wouldn't need to go to the hospital.

"And you know why they're going to be healthy?" Rebecca gazed around the classroom, her classmates squirming in their chairs, as she waited to get their full attention. It didn't come. Some were folding little pieces of paper into origamilike shapes. Most were talking to their neighbor.

Rebecca pushed on. She informed the class—future citizens of the Ideal City—of fruit trees planted by the thousands. If you were hungry, you could just pull off an orange.

"I hate oranges," Sylvia remarked.

"Then you can eat a peach. We'll have lots of peach trees."

Sylvia growled that she hated peaches, too, and was starting to list other fruit she despised when the loudspeaker crackled. Mrs. Lynch raised her face, her eyeglasses slipping from her nose but caught by the chain that held them.

The class became attentive, leaning their bodies toward the speaker, as if they wanted to hear another person's voice.

"Students, the freezer is broken again," Mr. Rafferty disclosed in a weak voice. He seemed out of breath, as if he had climbed a staircase and was taking a break at the landing.

No further explanation was required. The class roared, arms raised high, and were out of their chairs, some of them dancing and giving one another high fives. When Mrs. Lynch gave them the okay, they lined up against the wall. None of them pushed; for them this was the Ideal Moment.

While the students left in centipede fashion, Rebecca remained behind with Mrs. Marshall, the teacher's aide, who had papers to correct. She had told Mrs. Lynch that she wasn't hungry for ice cream and, anyhow, she had so much more to say about the Ideal City.

With the classroom empty the clock beat out its time. Rebecca regarded the chaos of sweaters hanging sloppily on the backs of chairs, the stains on the carpet, books shelved upside down: mess, mess, mess, everywhere.

She continued. "I have told you about the parks and the river," she told the desks. "I said that we would walk a lot. You know that. You also know that there will be bicycles, but I haven't said anything yet about skates. Skates can be dangerous if you decide to go down a mountain in them. But don't worry. I haven't ruled them out."

Rebecca stopped abruptly when she heard how her voice echoed off the walls with authority. She was impressed. She had imagined the dental hygienist as mayor, but she began to consider the position for herself.

"Now let me tell you, citizens!" The sentence echoed with drama. She giggled and thought, *I* really *like that. I sound so different.*

She then made her face serious and began again, aware of her posture as she stood soldier straight.

"Now let me tell you—you're going to hate this—but there will be no competitive sports. I know, I know, you like sports, but they have to stop."

She described the activities that would replace sports and pointed out a mountain range on the map. "See this mountain? It's green. It's green all the time because rain comes every three days. The flowers will die, but just for a couple of days; then they'll grow back. Yes, this is the mountain. No cars will go there because there won't be cars and no one will get parking tickets and stuff. We will walk—no, trek. We will trek up the mountain and right here—the place I'm touching on the picture—there's going to be a slide. You can slide down the mountain if you want."

Rebecca licked her lips. There was so much to say.

"You can slide down and go home. Everyone will have a home, and the dogs and cats will be happy. You will also get chickens to lay as many eggs as you want, and each house will come with two cows. It's going to be nice. Families will come in fours and no one will get sick. It's easy, really. This is the Ideal City. It will be clean, and there will be no cars—I said this already, I know, I know—but there will be no cars to make people angry, about parking tickets and stuff—I know, I know, I said that, too. You will walk and you will get into shape, or if you're already in shape, you'll get into better shape. You can climb the mountain or fish or just sit in the parks. The birds will sing different songs, and if you want, you can sing with them, like this."

Rebecca began a bird call, which had Mrs. Marshall peering up through her reading glasses. For the heck of it Rebecca crowed a cock-a-doodle-doo. She giggled with her hand over her mouth, but quickly reigned in her laughter when Mrs. Marshall shook her head.

"It's going to be nice," Rebecca announced as she paced in front of the classroom. She became serious, picked up the ruler, tapped her map, and maintained that everyone would be happy—the word *happy* echoed brightly off the wall. The desks, all in neat rows, all attentive, didn't once interrupt what she had to say about the ideal world.

D in English

RYAN GONZALEZ, twelve years old, was feeling under his bed for a sock that would match the brown one on his foot when his mother's angry voice reached his ears. "Ryan," she barked, "how could you get a D in English? No one born in this country gets a D in English!"

He could think of a dozen reasons, the most compelling that he had lost his textbook and the least compelling that the stuff they read in class was boring. His yawns were not big enough to convey his boredom. The poems and stories were sugar-coated lies. What was real was PlayStation 3. That he could get into.

When his mother's footsteps began pounding down the hallway, Ryan—a magician in such pinches—decided on a quick exit. Since he was already on his knees, he just lay flat on the clothes-littered floor and slid under the bed.

And just in time.

His mother pushed open the door and entered, roaring, "Ryan, I am tired of this!" She paused. Ryan imagined that she was sniffing the air like a blood-hound, as if she could pick up his scent. She pulled back the curtains and opened the window, muttering, "It smells in here."

Ryan placed a hand over his heart, which was beat-ing so hard he was convinced that she could hear it. And did his room really smell?

His mother stepped across the room and opened one of his drawers. *She's snooping,* he realized. *She's looking to see if I have drugs.* He stewed at her lack of trust. He would never do anything to harm his body, and this included his head. In truth, his head was dented in two places from falling out of trees. But he would never take drugs.

As he waited under the bed, he felt something at his side—it made a crinkly sound he was sure his mother had heard. Any second she would peer under the bed. What then? Smile? Maybe say, "Oh, I was looking for my Game Boy." Or perhaps he could get up, redden his face with anger, and snap, "Why did you come into my room without knocking? Why are you snooping in my drawers?"

But she didn't seem to have heard the crinkly sound of his hand touching whatever it was. The territory under his bed was a graveyard of lost things, including unwashed socks.

After his mother left, closing the door softly behind her, Ryan crawled out. He looked down at the object that had nearly given him away: a Snickers candy bar. He wondered how long it had been under the bed. Since Halloween? Halloween the year before? It didn't matter. He tore the wrapper open with his teeth and took a healthy bite. The candy was old, but the flavor sweetened the moment.

Ryan checked to see if his mother had taken anything from his drawer. He stopped the laborious chewing of the old candy bar, touched by what he discovered. His mother had rolled his white gym socks and underwear into tidy balls. He admonished himself for thinking that his mother was a snoop.

Still, Ryan figured he'd better get out of the house before he got into trouble that Saturday morning. He located a sock for his bare foot, a blue one that contrasted with the brown one. He slipped into shoes and a Fresno State hoodie. He opened his bedroom door and, Ninjalike, peeked out before he hurried down the hallway. His mother, he judged from the noise in the kitchen, was loading the dishwasher.

Out the front door and down the steps, he hurdled over the rosebushes, dislodging a few petals. He looked back. Would his mother be angrier that he had ruined a beautiful red rose or that he had chiseled a D in English into his academic record? But he didn't have time for this debate. He scurried away, the spring air rushing about his ears and combing his hair into odd angles.

Where should I go? he asked himself. He thought of his friend Freddie Fernandez, but remembered that Freddie was sentenced to wash all three of his family's beat-up cars, plus mow the lawn, and who knew what else. Like Ryan, Freddie had gotten a D in English— and worse, a D in Spanish. His Mexican parents could not understand how their son, born in that south-of-the-border country, could do so poorly at his *own* language.

Ryan thought, *I know. I'll go down to the lot.* The lot was where he, Freddie, and countless others hung out. It was a weedy patch of ground where they played soc-cer in the fall and baseball from March until the start of school in September. It was a place where he had wit-nessed a boy his own age kiss a girl right on the lips!

But when he got there, he discovered two boys hunkered over what appeared to be a motor. They were trying to pry it open with Popsicle sticks. To Ryan they resembled chimps poking sticks down ant holes.

"What are you chimps doing?" Ryan asked.

The two gazed up. Their hands were black from motor oil, and the corners of their mouths were black, too, from the licorice whips they had been eating.

"We found this thing," one explained. "The copper is like gold."

"Like gold," Ryan repeated. He didn't know much about electrical gizmos but imagined that the spool of copper made the small motor run by magnetic force or something—or was it that the copper cooled the motor? "What are you going to do with it?"

"Sell it," the second kid said with a snarl.

"And who's going to buy it?"

"Who's going to buy it?" the first kid repeated as he stood up. "The people who buy gold."

Ryan left the vacant lot thinking that those kids were even more vacant. Was he ever that dumb? He pushed his hands into his pockets and searched for money—he needed fifty cents for a soda from the vending machine outside Safeway. He could only locate a quarter and two dimes.

He began his trek to Safeway, hoping he could find five more cents on the way. He hadn't gotten very far when he had to hide behind a car. He'd spotted Travis Clark, a bully from school. There was no telling if Travis might jam him up for money or push him around just because it was something to do.

As Ryan waited behind the car, he searched the ground around him for a nickel. But he stiffened as a gravelly voice bellowed, "Get away from my car." Ryan looked in the direction of a small house—or did the house just look really small because the man on the porch was exceptionally large? The man, in his own Fresno State hoodie, grinned meanly at Ryan.

Yikes, Ryan thought. The guy had anvils for arms, and his neck was as thick as the motor the two fool boys had been trying to pry open. His grin spread and revealed a coppery grill.

"I was just—" began Ryan.

The man told him to shut up and get away from his car. Ryan didn't have to be told again. In an impromptu disguise he pulled up his hood and ran away with his head down, aware that he had left his fingerprints behind on the fender. Would the man call the police? No, Ryan felt that this guy was the type to settle matters on his own.

"It's Travis's fault," he muttered. "If he hadn't shown up, that guy wouldn't be growling at me." But he knew the blame was weak. He was just lurking behind a car, and the owner had resorted to threats. Boys his age responded to threats.

Ryan jogged until he was finally in front of Safeway, a touchstone of safety. He caught his breath and brought out the forty-five cents. He pounded on the vending machine, hoping it might burp a nickel or—this had happened before—a free soda. But the machine gave up nothing. His pounding just started the motor.

"Stupid machine," Ryan muttered. When he turned, he saw his mother exiting the store with two bags in her arms, struggling to keep the bags from slipping. He considered running over to help her, but he played it safe and lowered himself behind a car. He couldn't risk the public humiliation of his mother bawling him out about the D in English.

"Now who in the world is that?" he muttered.

A boy had approached his mother and taken one of the bags from her. She smiled at him in a way she never beamed at Ryan, her only son. She said something that made them both laugh. Ryan's jealousy grew when his mother set the groceries in the backseat, opened her purse, and pressed money into this do-gooder's palm.

The do-gooder protested and returned the money. She smiled at him and then, leaning into the car, brought out a soda from one of the bags.

"That's mine," Ryan murmured. He narrowed his eyes at the boy and hurried away, ashamed—no, mad. Who was that kid, anyway? And why was the kid helping Ryan's mother? That was *his* duty.

Ryan decided to head over to Freddie's house. He found his friend on his knees in front of his father's big old Chevy station wagon. He looked like he was praying before the old clunker, but he was actually scrubbing a tire with an old toothbrush.

"Hey," Ryan greeted. He picked up the garden hose, which was running on the lawn.

"My mom better not see you," Freddie said cautiously. He looked toward the front window of the house.

Ryan lowered his face to the hose and drank. With dribbles of water falling from his chin, he asked, "Why?"

"She thinks you're the reason I got a D in English *and* Spanish."

"Me?" Ryan pointed at his chest.

"Yeah!" Freddie snarled. "Now get over here, dude—don't stand on the lawn." With his chin he motioned for Ryan to hide behind the station wagon, which had decals on the back window that read ZACATECAS.

"Hey, isn't your last name Fernandez?" Ryan wondered.

"It is," Freddie said.

"Then how come you got that word Zaca-something on your window?"

Freddie clicked his tongue. "You don't know nothing. That's where my family is from."

"Oh," Ryan muttered. "I thought you were from Mexico."

Freddie repeated, "You don't know nothing."

Ryan shrugged and squatted next to Freddie, who had taken the toothbrush to the next tire.

"Man, I didn't do your homework," Ryan said as he returned to Freddie's complaint.

"I know that," Freddie said. "Mom just thinks it's your fault because you're a bad influence." His eyes shifted to Ryan's mismatched socks. "Man, your *calcetines* are all mixed up."

Licking his lips, Ryan was about to update Freddie on his poor choice of socks when Freddie's mother pushed open the screen door with her hip and came out with a pot in her hands. She said something in Spanish that Ryan couldn't understand. But Freddie knew: His mother needed help. He dropped the toothbrush as Ryan quickly wiggled under the car. He lay with his hands over his heart and listened to Freddie's mother say more in Spanish and—was it possible?—banter his name around. He thought he made out "Ryan, Ryan," but it might have been "Iran, Iran." But why would Freddie's mother be speaking to her son about the Middle East?

Freddie opened the car door for his mother, who sat in the passenger side with the pot in her lap. The car squeaked under her weight. Ryan worried that Freddie's father was about to come down the stairs, too. And he did.

What should I do? Ryan wondered. He considered gripping the underside of the car when it started to move. He had seen the maneuver in a movie about a criminal terrorizing a law-abiding family. But that criminal was superstrong, and Ryan had to admit that he was noodle-armed.

When Freddie's father plopped himself into the driver's seat, Ryan wisely decided it was time to escape. He rolled out, duck-walked along the side of the car below the window level, and left a trail of fingerprints before he rose and ran away. He didn't look back, didn't quip *Adiós, amigo* to Freddie.

Once out of sight, Ryan meandered slowly to the playground, but paused when he saw Travis the bully on a motorized scooter. A smaller boy ran after him, crying. One day when Travis had pushed him around, Ryan had gotten a D on a math quiz and had been so troubled he forgot to do his English homework. Travis, Ryan convinced himself, was the reason sixth grade was not turning out to be a good year.

He stole it, Ryan figured. He leaned into a tree and, when Travis spotted him, wished he had climbed into it. Travis made a loopy circle, let the scooter fall in the road, and advanced toward Ryan while running a comb through his hair.

"Fool, what you doing?" Travis greeted. He ran a thumb down the comb.

"Nothing, man." Ryan pushed himself away from the tree. "I'm looking for . . . fruit." He raised his eyes toward the network of limbs.

"Fool, you think I'm a fool? That's a sycamore. No fruit." He put the comb into his back pocket.

Ryan swallowed. He shifted his attention to the scooter that the smaller boy had righted. Shoulders heaving, the boy was dropping dime-sized tears on the black asphalt and gunning down the street. Ryan pointed. "Look, the little man's stealing your ride."

Travis smiled. "Gonzalez, you weenie." He hooked a thumb at the boy. "That's my brother. I ought to hit you."

"You already did that. Twice." Ryan began to re-count the times in fourth and fifth grades, but Travis advised him to shut up. He was in a hurry. He plunged one of his hands into Ryan's pocket and pulled out the forty-five cents.

"Is that all you got?" Travis asked.

"Yeah," Ryan answered weakly.

"I ought to smack you one." He wagged his head. "I can't believe you got a D in English."

"How do you know?"

"Everyone knows. You and that ugly dude Freddie. You're bringing the male species down."

Ryan almost uttered, "Are we a species? I thought only animals were species," but he ground the words on the back of his molars. He thought, *Just keep your trap closed.*

Travis flipped a dime and slapped it against his wrist. "Heads or tails."

"Heads," Ryan guessed.

When Travis brought his hand away, it was heads. "You're right, but you still lose." He sneered at Ryan and lumbered off, hitching up his pants.

Bullies, Ryan assumed, didn't get grades higher than Cs. But as he walked down the street, pockets no longer jingling with coins, he remembered that Travis had been the spelling bee champ in fourth and fifth grade and had taken a test that suggested he was a genius. *Sweet,* Ryan thought. *To be strong and smart, plus know the names of trees!*

"Dang, I'm thirsty," Ryan complained. "I could use a soda." Still, he didn't dare return home. His mother would turn up the fires of anger and roast his ears with accusations about laziness. He walked aimlessly toward downtown and soon found himself near the library.

"They got a drinking fountain there," he told himself.

As he entered, Ryan was happily surprised by the cool air. It was only April, but the weather was already warm—and his foxlike running about didn't help. He wished he could strip off his hoodie, but decided that decency was required in a public place.

He found the drinking fountain, then spent time looking at a large globe of the world. He spun it, closed his eyes, and let his finger trail the surface until it stopped, telling himself, *This is where I'm going to die.* He opened his eyes and lowered his face to read where he would die, in old age, of course: Estonia. Ryan had never heard of the country. He spun the globe again to get an answer he liked better when he spotted a familiar face.

"It's that dude," he muttered. Ryan was sure it was the boy who had helped his mother with the groceries, who had drunk what was *his* soda, and who may have taken his place in his mother's heart. Ryan approached the boy, who was stuffing papers into his backpack.

"You're the one, huh?" Ryan asked.

The boy's large, luminous eyes fell on Ryan. He shrugged the backpack onto his shoulder and fit a small pencil into his shirt pocket. "I'm the one, what?"

"Who helped my mom at Safeway," Ryan answered.

"Mrs. Gonzalez?" the boy said brightly.

"Yeah," Ryan answered and gritted his teeth. The word *yeah,* usable in the streets, suddenly sounded stupid in the library. No wonder he got a D in English.

"She's very nice," the boy said seriously. He introduced himself as Gregorio Mendez. He told Ryan he had to go to his tutoring job and invited him to see his class.

"What class?"

"The ESL class," Gregorio answered. "I'll show you."

Gregorio walked down the hall with long, sharp, and purposeful steps. Ryan followed, noticing that his own steps were scrambled; his feet were splayed like a duck's and his shoelaces whipped about like skinny snakes.

"I've been tutoring for three months," Gregorio

said. An idea sparked in Ryan's mind: *Hey, maybe he can help me.* But he discarded the idea. He couldn't see himself being tutored by a kid smaller than he was.

"It's a special day," Gregorio whispered. He began to tiptoe as they got closer to the classroom.

"What do you mean?" Ryan found himself tiptoeing as well.

Gregorio didn't answer and prodded Ryan into the classroom. Ryan stalled like a stubborn donkey. His hair, sweaty from running around, nearly bristled when he spotted Freddie Fernandez's mom in the front row.

Gregorio bowed his head slightly at the teacher, and Ryan, not knowing what to do, did the same. Shaken by the presence of Freddie's mom, he followed Gregorio timidly to the back of the room. He considered lifting his hood over his head, but decided to be brave.

"Mrs. Fernandez," the teacher said in a jolly voice.

Freddie's mom rose. There was applause from her classmates as she seemed to cha-cha-cha to the front. She gazed briefly at Ryan, and her smile, already wide, seemed to get even bigger. She didn't seem mad at Ryan for supposedly bringing down Freddie's grades. Had Freddie been making it all up?

"Your certificate," the teacher said. "Excellence in English. Congratulations." Mrs. Fernandez took the certificate, shook hands with her teacher, smiled at the class, and returned to her seat in a hail of applause.

Ryan felt weak. He took a seat and listened to the names of the certificate winners: Nui Ying Yang, Soon Kim, Hikari Oda, Thalia Kisro, Michaela Liedkate, the husband-and-wife team of Samuel and Ester Ortiz, a dozen others from faraway countries but mostly from Latin America. Each of them pranced to the front of the class to accept their certificates.

"Now for the real reason why we're here," the teacher said. He jokingly glanced over at the potluck food on a long table. He rubbed his stomach and asked the class, "What are we?"

"We are hungry," the students said in a variety of accents. They rose, some beginning to speak in their native languages.

Everyone appeared happy as they got into two lines. Ryan was amazed. At school he would have crowded to the front or begged a friend to let him cut. He looked down at the desk, embarrassed. He was born in this country and a native speaker of English; how could he get a D? And these people? They worked hard all week and came to study English on Saturday afternoons.

"Come on," Gregorio urged. "Let's get in line."

"Nah, I ain't hungry," Ryan said. He twiddled his

fingers for a few seconds, and then clicked his tongue. *I got to grow up,* he admonished himself. *Maybe I'm what Travis called me: a fool!* He pushed his hands into his pockets and then brought them out. He fiddled with his hood and crossed his arms across his chest. He couldn't find a comfortable position.

"This is for you, *mi'jo,*" Freddie's mom beckoned as she came toward him. She held two plates brimming with Chinese and Filipino food. Her smile revealed a gold tooth.

He swallowed and felt tenderness toward her. "Thank you," he said, and meant it. He sat up and smiled as he took the plate with both hands.

"You and Freddie are like this." She crossed her one finger over another. "So close. *Amigos.*" Ryan was glad that she didn't say anything about their Ds in English.

Freddie's mom lifted a *lumpia* with chopsticks and nibbled. "All you have to do is eat different to be somewhere different."

"It's true," Ryan agreed, though he wasn't sure what she meant.

Freddie's mom continued to talk in English about a two-for-one sale at Target, and he nodded after each completed sentence. He didn't mind that it went long, that she sometimes changed the subject to Freddie, that her grammar was shaky. No, he wanted to encourage her, to tell her with his eyes and smile that she was all right.

Ryan had experienced a growing spurt the previous summer. He was now taller than his mother and almost as tall as his father. That day Ryan had another kind of growth. He could no longer play like a little kid in a vacant lot. He had to dust the dirt from his pants, tie his shoes, and stride in long, meaningful steps. He had to walk as a young man.

Selected Spanish Words and Phrases

ay, dios mio: oh, my god

bueno: hello (when answering the telephone)

calcetines: socks

cállate: shut up

camarones para mi: shrimp for me

"Canción de mi Vida": a song; means "song of my life"

chamacos: kids

churro: a type of doughnut

"Cielito Lindo": a popular Mariachi song; means "beautiful little sky"

claro qué sí: of course

comadre: very close female friend

como lata: what a bother

día: day

menudo: a traditional Mexican soup

mercado: market

mi abuelito: my grandpa

la migra: U.S. immigration officials, such as the
Border Patrol

mi'ja/mi'jo: my daughter/son

nada: nothing

nalgas: buttocks

no es Luis Miguel, pero es okay: it's not Luis Miguel,
but it's okay

oye: hey

puro: complete

que horible: how horrible

qué quieres, mi cielo: what do you want, my heaven

ranchito: a small ranch

tres días de: three days of

tu sabes: you know

Vamos a comer comida Mexicana en un restaurante:
We are going to eat Mexican food in a restaurant

vámanos: let's go

vieja/viejo: old woman/man

GARY SOTO's first book for young readers, *Baseball in April and Other Stories,* was a breakout book in literature about Latino young people. He has since published many novels, short stories, plays, and poetry collections for adults and children. Mr. Soto divides his time between Berkeley, California, and his hometown of Fresno in California's San Joaquin Valley.

www.garysoto.com